# The Burberry Style:
## An Enigma-wrapped Mystery

❖

A Balona Book
by
## Jonathan Pearce

ISBN 0-7414-0969-0

*Published by:*

**INFINITY**
PUBLISHING.COM

*519 West Lancaster Avenue*
*Haverford, PA 19041-1413*
*Info@buybooksontheweb.com*
*www.buybooksontheweb.com*
*Toll-free (877) BUY BOOK*
*Local Phone (610) 520-2500*
*Fax (610) 519-0261*

∞

*Printed in the United States of America*

*Printed on Recycled Paper*

*Published February, 2002*

In memory of Coach Bob Long,
generous, humorous, tough,
smart, caring, kind.

# 1

## Simon Burberry

The assassins pursuing me are probably two in number. It is possible there are three, the third unknown to the pair—known in tradecraft as an "insurance agent." They will likely try to sneak up on me when I am least prepared to confront them. They will probably use the *garrotte* or high-impact plastic knives, as firearms are now so much more difficult to move through international airlines. In any event they will likely need to get close.

If I hadn't been in such a cowardly dither about my personal safety, I would not have lost the case in such a foolish manner. I had been glancing in the rear-view mirror frequently and had thus missed the turn-off to the Interstate. I found myself on a country road, little traveled evidently, except by large gray lorries laden with bits of gravel that blew off and struck my windscreen again and again.

The road sign, white letters on a green background, read "Balona, A Friendly Place," and I presumed that in this little hamlet I could acquire enough petrol to see me on my way safely via back roads. I would thus not have to worry about murderous agents sent by Lady Demelza's swinish suitor, at least for a time.

I crossed a bridge over a trickle of stream labeled "Yulumne River," saw a petrol sign on my left, turned round-about in the middle of the street and pulled into the station. Building needed a fresh coat of paint. Petrol pumps hadn't been wiped clean in perhaps years. Office window filthy. I was almost atremble with indignation. The help nowadays, anywhere, is truly atrocious.

A short stout youth was polishing a motorcycle next to the pump. "Clean my windscreen, if you please," I said politely. He barely looked up from his task.

"I don't please. You pay in there first. Then you can clean your own damn window." This was my initiation, my welcome to Balona, A Friendly Place.

I did as I was told and paused to select a handful of picture postcards from a fly-blown display just inside the door. "Vistas of Balona" read the sign at the top of the rack. Upon close inspection the cards were of scenes circa 1955 and featured Front Street buildings in sepia-tone. Nevertheless, I needed the cards to keep the connection with dear Mum open. A surly youth inside, a boy with fire-red pimples, took my currency and turned away without giving me change. "My change, please."

"Change? You give me a ten, and you, like, get them cards in your hand and nine dollars of gas. So, like, go get it. You don't get no change. I don't keep change on account of muggers and stuff."

While filling the tank, I set my case upon the top of the car and got out the road map, being careful to lock the case, even for such a brief occasion. My caution was based on recent experience when I had left the case on the same roof under similar circumstances and drove off with it teetering there. Fortunately, I have always kept my boxes in the boot, so there is little chance of their becoming lost unless I should lose the car. I chuckled at the thought of someone's finding my boxes and the puzzlement at how one might open them!

Balona looked as if it had died.

"So this is Balona, a friendly place," I said, again attempting to initiate friendly banter with the young motorcycle-polishing citizen.

No response.

"Have you a hotel in Balona."

"Burnt down last year."

"Well, are there rooms to let, perhaps?"

"To let what?"

"Ah, to rent. Rooms for rent."

"Ask at Kuhl's Real Estate. Over there on Front Street."

"That would be...?"

"Yeh." The youth completed his cosmetic chore, climbed on his cycle, and sped off in a cloud of smoke, fog, and dust.

I decided Balona was truly not the friendly place it advertised itself to be, and that I should seek the Interstate and thence another location in which to disappear. With that and lost in thought I replaced the petrol hose, climbed in my vehicle, and returned the way I had come—at perhaps a faster clip than that at which I had arrived. The fog-fuzzy sun was beginning to set and masses of insects thrashed themselves against the glass. I noticed that I had forgotten to clean the windscreen. I wondered if I had remembered to replace the fuel tank cap.

I was half-way to the Interstate, whistling to myself, when it occurred to me that my case was not on the seat next to me. I had again left it on the roof of the car. "Blast!" I exclaimed. I stopped at once, but of course, the case was gone. It had slipped off somewhere between my present location and the service station in Balona.

I determined to retrieve the case at once, for it contained not only most of my funds, and my access to the rest, but also papers of momentous import, a treasured photograph, my vocabulary builder, Uncle Sweeney's best razor (an heirloom), my swagger stick, my flask of English Leather, clean Argylles, et cetera.

I watched the roadside carefully, slowing down significantly to do so, thereby evidently creating some bit of havoc among the lorry drivers sounding their klaxons behind me. Red and blue lights in my rear-view mirror stimulated me to pull entirely off the roadway. Soon a stout fellow in uniform approached. I lowered the window.

"Had a couple too many, have ya?" The round red nose twitched. Beady eyes searched the interior of my vehicle.

"Sir?"

"Been at the brewski in Mello Fello Pizza, have ya?"

"Pardon?"

"You been drinking, have ya?" The fellow wore a silver metal star on his dark-blue bosom and a large white cowboy hat with a hole in the crown. The hole was edged with dark gray. It appeared that it might be a bullet hole. I was in the Far West at last. John Wayne Country perhaps, although a weatherbeaten sign at the side of the road testified that this was *Carp Country*. Some wag had attacked the letters of the first word with a marking pen. John Wayne spoke again: "You're driving slower than the flow of traffic and you're on the wrong side of the road."

Betrayed by custom! Of course, in Britain one drives on the left-hand side of the road, and there I was on the left-hand side again in a right-hand-side world. I at once created a cover story for the constable. "I'm a scientist looking for specimens, sir."

"Oh, well, then. That's okay. I guess you're a foreigner, too?" He had discerned my origins, possibly in my accent.

"Yes, an anthropologist." I smiled at my quick creativity.

"Oh, yeh. Sure. Birds. Well, we got plenty around here. You find any?"

"No, I'm losing the light, y'know."

"Well, good luck, but get on the other side of the road," said the officer, readying himself for departure. "Dumb foreigner," he muttered to himself but loud enough for the rudeness to be overheard. Aloud: "You more like to find samples on the West Levee Road. Anybody knows that. Oh, well, it's a free country." He turned and fumbled in his shirt pocket, brought forth a large red plastic button printed with a photo and the legend *Anson Chaud for Sheriff* in white letters. "Here, you wear this and it's as good as a stay–out-of-jail card, ha ha ha, since I'm this guy here." He licked his thumb and wiped the photo with it before he handed it to me. The sheriff's voice was high and he lisped. He also walked as if his cowboy boots might be pinching. He drove off, sounding a brief *woop* on his siren as he departed.

After fastening the button to my coat lapel, I penned some notes about the experience on a 3x5 card found on the floor of the car. I fervently wished for my notebooks, now reposing in the lost briefcase. That thought reminded me of the pre-eminence of my mission, and I returned to examining the roadside, with more speed now but no success.

With the setting of the sun I realized I must find some place to rest, else I would need to spend another night in the car. I decided against returning to the Interstate and seeking a roadside motel, for such establishments would be among the first places the assassins would look. Inhospitable Balona would have to do.

I turned on my headlamps after a vehicle passed me on the right, sounding its horn vigorously, the driver shouting something and gesticulating rudely with a finger. I had slipped into old habits and was again driving on the left-hand side of the road. Smiling ironically, I realized that if I were not more careful, I would be completing Mr. Tudwick's very aim: to do away with me. If only Lady Demelza had been able to explain to the high-tempered fellow.

Balona seemed to be if not dead, then asleep already, its main thoroughfare dimly lighted, its businesses closed, its advertising limited to a flashing furry red and green neon announcement of *Hannibal Chaud's Funerals*. But several establishments midblock emitted pale yellow shafts of light through the fog. The sidewalks were dark and wet.

I parked and locked the car, strode across the street into Frank's Soupe de Jour, pausing only to drop another airmail postcard in the curbside box—one of my many frantic apologies to Mum. The postboxes in this country are blue, and more difficult to notice in the fog than the fine noticeably red boxes of Britain. I sat at the counter, and ordered coffee. A very tall fellow wearing a soiled apron served me. The embroidery on his shirt pocket declaimed the frayed name *Frank*.

"I'm famished. What's good to eat?"

"Well, uh, my, y'know, Franksburger is, y'know, great."

"What is that gentleman having?" I pointed discreetly at the eager wolfings of an elderly bloke.

"Well, uh, that's, y'know, a korndog."

"I'll have one of those, please." The item appeared vaguely similar to a solo toad-in-the-hole, but neater. Comfortingly familiar image on a dark wet afternoon in a strange land.

"Korndogs in Balona don't got no stick, y'know. They just lay there."

I was taken unawares by this piece of intelligence, but I only shrugged, not knowing what to make of it.

"I mean, y'know, you don't pick up a Balona korndog, like a corndog somewheres else, or like one of my fine Franksburgers. No, it just lays there, y'know, on the plate."

"I see. It does. Well, that's certainly interesting. I'll have two."

"Yeh, well, suit yourself. You working for, y'know, Anson Chaud, are you?"

"The sheriff was kind enough to provide this button."

"Yeh, well, just for your information the election it'n until next month."

"Ah. Is there a motel near here, sir?" I could hear myself reverting to my subservient habits of speech.

"Motel 6 at the end of the West Levee Road. Maybe five miles west." He wiped at the counter with a grossly soiled rag. I could smell the grease but resisted offering advice as to how he might fold the cloth so as to gain more use of the cleaner surfaces of the fabric.

"Nothing in Balona?"

"You could ast Kenworth Kuhl, down the street." He snickered in his chest, joined in the snicker by the two elderly men at the counter also consuming korndogs and drinking coffee.

"Everything looks closed."

"Everybody's saving on lights is why. You just go on down there and, y'know, try the door. I betcha there's, y'know, somebody in there right now. It's only four-thirty or so. Everything, y'know, should be open till five."

The korndog was superb. Much, much superior to our banger. The coffee was execrable. I was reminded of Mum's coffee and my eyes misted.

"What is the composition of this sauce, please? It's quite, mm, piquant. Very flavourful. Travels so well with the, mm, korndog."

"Travels, yeh, well, it's, y'know, a secret sauce. I mean, y'know, we don't, y'know, tell strangers the, y'know, recipe." Frank did not smile,

"Ah. Pity. It is jolly good, y'know." I showed my teeth, paid (including a small tip, always appreciated by those in service), thanked Frank for his kind attention, and trudged down the street to Kenworth Kuhl Real Estate. The door was indeed open and I entered, hoping to find a friendly face in this forsaken place.

# 2

## Joseph Oliver Kuhl

"Burberry. Simon Burberry." The tall sinister-looking stranger introduced himself and stated his business through his teeth with his mouth not quite open. You also got the impression he was looking under his black hatbrim out of the corner of his eyes behind his wrap-around dark glasses. This optional feature was sort of strange since the sun was down already and Front Street was under its usual February fog. Also, we were standing inside *Kenworth Kuhl Real Estate & Joseph O. Kuhl Private Investigations* with some of the lights off to save on the PG&E bill. Actually, I was sitting. He was standing, his trench coat tied suavely, not buttoned. He had on a yellow plaid scarf, one end hanging out of the trench coat top. He had one of Uncle Anson's buttons on his left lapel. On his left wrist he was wearing a gold watch that he kept looking at.

I went, "Burbley?" trying to match his pronunciation.

"Burberry," he repeated. "English, y'know."

"Yes, Burble. I heard you." The English sort of mess up their pronunciation so you can't really hear what they're saying. "You got a first name, too?"

"Just Burberry." He took off his hat very carefully, put it on the corner of my desk, smoothed his black hair down with his palms. He removed his shades and stuffed them inside his coat.

"Just Burble. Now there's an interesting name. Maybe short for *Justice*, I guess. So, Just, how come you picked on Balona to hang out in?"

Squinted eyes, suspicious look. "Why do you inquire?"

"Interested in newcomers since I write a sort of column for the paper once and a while and could use some copy."

"I am not seeking 'copy,' dear boy. In fact, I would prefer no attention be paid me at all."

"How so's that?"

"I'm working under cover."

"All right! You're FBI. No, NSA. No, CIA."

"MI-6"

"Wow! All right!" I happened to know already that MI-6 is British Secret Service.

Eyebrow up, steel-gray eyes narrowed. "You *know* MI-6?"

"Sure, I intend to join up over there myself, soon as I get my diploma, my certificate from C4. That's Chaud County Community College."

"Oh, yes?" There's a twitching at the left-hand corner of Mr. Burble's mustache, a growth sort of like Saddam Hussein's of TV fame.

"Criminal Justice, Just." I smirked at the confluence of names, also pleased at last to find a use, even interminably, for one of Doctor Fardel's usually useless vocabulary words like *confluence*.

"I see. Well, refer to me simply as Mr. Burberry, if you please." Mr. Burberry was lost in thought for a few seconds, looking at the ceiling. "Or you might address me as *Commander* Burberry when we're alone." He raised both eyebrows, put a mean look on his face.

The English are so formal, getting pushed out of shape right away about calling them by their first name. The way he said stuff sounded suave, though, even though most of it came through his nose. I think I will try the accent out on Patella and Millie and maybe Willow. See what they think before I adopt it as my style.

"So, okay. Where you staying right now, Commander?"

"You need to know that."

"Well, you're looking for a place to stay, so when my dad comes back from his nap, his research, over at Frings Bowls, I could get in touch with you."

"Yes. I see. Well, don't worry about that. I'll be in touch with *you.* You say there's a house for rent and rooms for rent. Does the house face east?" Commander Burberry was writing on a 3x5 card while looking at me over the tops of his eyes.

I thought for a minute, turned in my chair to several directions, ponderating. "No, it faces north." I didn't mention that my dad wasn't exactly the agent for it, either. Probably the house didn't have an agent, so that was okay.

"North is not good. Should face the sunrise."

"Old lady Crinkle's place faces south, I think. Or maybe north. Or east, maybe. I forget. She's looking for a roomer, since her daughter moved off and Mr. Keyshot moved out. Nice clean room, they say. Old lady been around forever. Probably mind her own binnis."

"Old lady, you said. How old?"

"Well, maybe 95, 98, something like that. Old. But she can take care of herself all right. Strong as an ox, they say. Actually a relative of mine."

"Ah. Well, give me the address and I'll swing by there and give it a look-see."

"Is that a Ferrari you're driving out there?" The car was low, blue or black. I couldn't tell in the fog but in the dim light shining on it from Peking Peek-Inn the car looked pretty racy.

"It's an Aston-Martin."

"Wow. Like James Bond."

"Of course." He raised an eyebrow and reached inside his trench coat for his cigaret case. Gold, too. He snapped it open, plucked out a cigaret, tapped it on the case. Put it back in the case, and put the case back inside his coat. "Quit smoking, y'know."

"Yeh, me, too." I never did smoke, but in Balona you are expected to show how suave you are, even to strangers, so sometimes you have to lie a little. Kind of like guys who sport cowboy hats who never saw a cow in their life. Or guys who wear Air Jordans who never lifted their butt off of the couch. It occurred to me that this secret agent might very well be on a case. He looked like a secret agent on a case. He acted like a secret agent in action. He probably even smelled like one. "Say, you aren't a secret agent on a case, are you?"

He raised one eyebrow again. The same one. Twitched his lip. Then raised both eyebrows. "Who knows. If I told you I'd have to kill you." He raised one side of his lip again in what I guess was a smile.

"Wow." I couldn't help admiring how suave he was. I couldn't help letting my admiration show.

"The address of both house and room, young sir?"

I gave him both, which I wrote by hand on the back of one of my business cards.

He squinted at the addresses and turned over the card. The eyebrows rose up again. "This is you? You are an actual private detective?"

I stood there with my mouth hanging open for a while, trying to figure out what "ake-shl" meant. Then I figured it out. "Yeh, ake-

9

shl. The only one in Balona." I worried about the legal part, maybe lying to a real secret agent, so I gave him the usual script. "Not quite certified yet, though, since I'm still in school, y'know. C4? Chaud County Community College? That's where I'm learning criminal justice."

"Memorable card." He looked at my original design and the several expensive colors and different styles of type, and specially the magpie up in the corner, rubbing at it and getting some of the ink on his thumb. He blinked several times, as if he was having eye problems. He looked definitely sinister, blinking like that.

So I had a thought. "It's getting pretty dark, y'know. No old lady's gonna open the door to a stranger with a black hat and a mustache around here. So you're sort of out of luck for tonight. But we got a cot back there." I jerked my thumb at the back room where we store cardboard boxes, stuff my dad collects and doesn't dare take home, and an old army cot where Dad sleeps when Ma has thrown him out of the house. "The cot's vacant tonight."

Mr. Burberry looked at me and squinted his eyes. "Very good of you. Very, uh, neighborly."

"Well, it's not much. And it won't cost you much, either." No sense in letting a good cot go to waste when you got a rube right at hand ready to pay for it. Even a secret agent is a rube in Balona until he wises up. That's the Balona spirit.

"I see. You expect to charge me for the cot."

"Well, it's sort of insurance, y'know, since me and Dad will be going home and leaving you here with my computer and important documents and stuff. Besides it's only, uh, ten bucks."

"Ten dollars for the cot."

"No, for the night. We keep the cot."

He peeled off a bill from a huge cash roll he took out of his pocket. "There are facilities back there?" He meant, was there a toilet.

"Well, not exactly. Usually, we go next door in the daytime, so if you gotta go at night, well, it's dark back there and, y'know, you just open the door and, you know."

The door popped open and Mr. Burberry, his back to the door, jumped like he'd been goosed. It was only Dad who came in looking startled, as usual. Dad's red-headed dog Killer came in, too, shook himself and flopped down under Dad's desk. Right away the whole room started smelling like wet dog. Mr.

Burberry's nose twitched. Dad went, "A client for you, Joey?" Dad hasn't had a client all year so I suppose he thought Commander Burberry was my client.

"A client for *you*, Dad. Mr. Burble."

Dad searched for his comb in his shirt pocket, swiped his thin fog-wet tan hair and scraped it through his mustache where there isn't enough hair to need combing. "Pleased to meet you, Mr. Burble."

Mr. Burberry bowed his head. "Sir," he went. Then he looked up at the ceiling and frowned, like he'd maybe committed a peccadildo by bowing.

"We should get Mr. Burble a chair to sit on, Joey, uh, Joe."

I moved a chair so Mr. Burberry could sit, and he did, stretching his legs out so his checkered socks showed. Shiny shoes, like a dancer. Maybe the Commander made his public living on the stage. "Do you dance, Mr. Burble?"

He made a strangled sound, like a horse laughing in his nose. "Only when asked, and then not well."

"Maybe you should take Mr. Burble's coat, Joey, uh, Joe."

"I told Mr. Burble he could sleep in our back room there, on the cot."

"How so?"

"Well, you're not gonna use it tonight, I thought, so I..."

"Mr. Burble should come home with us and stay the night in the rec room. We can fix him up with a rental in the morning when he can visit around and decide for himself."

"My word," went Mr. Burberry. "I wouldn't wish to impose on your hospitality, sir."

"No indispose at all, you don't mind home-cooked food."

I began to worry about that, since my ma is the worst cook in Chaud County. "We could take home some Peking Peek-Inn takeout, Dad."

"Maybe we better, son. Yes, let's do that. Mr. Burble, did you see a magpie up on the roof here when you came in?"

"It's Burberry, sir. It was already rather dark and..."

"Oh, well. He's there sometimes. Sometimes he's not. You never know with magpies."

Dad has this thing about a magpie he sees, even when it's not there. Nobody else sees it, either, especially in February when magpies are gone off to warmer places. Dad needs some help, maybe, so I put a magpie picture on my business card like a good son, to give him some self-esteem. Besides, magpies are known to collect stuff, the way a good PI collects information. So the magpie is a good motto.

Dad gathered a handful of pencils from his desk drawer, looked around the office, scratched his head, put the pencils back in the drawer. "Well, I guess we can do it right now. Joey, you go ahead and get us a mess of chop suey over there, on the tab, and bring it on home, and I'll take Mr. Burble with me."

"Burberry, sir. I can follow you in my own vehicle. This is very gracious of you, sir. I had no idea Balona would be so gracious." He gave me a steely look, so I handed him his 10 dollars back, money I had plans for. "By the by," he said to me sort of confidentially, "Have you seen any strange people in Balona recently?"

"Only Mr. Carp. He's pretty strange."

"Mr. Carp?"

"He's our grocer. And my dad there. He's even stranger."

The Commander snorted in his nose, put his black hat back on and left, searching in all his pockets for something, muttering to himself.

Actually, I remember he said his first name was Simon, not Just. Commander Burberry must have been trying to confuse me the way secret agents will do.

# 3

## Joseph O. Kuhl

The briefcase was bigger and thicker than a regular briefcase and made out of purplish leather. It had gold hinges and latches. It had the initials SB in gold on it in gold letters. It looked like it was owned by a rich guy, what with the gold initials. I wondered how my Cousin Zack had got a hold of it. I needed to lubricate the way since Zack is sort of self-centered, so I mentioned, suavely, "Hey, Zack. *Klaatu barada nikto!*"

"Yeh, yeh."

Zack I guess is bored of stuff from old movies. "How'd you get a hold of this thing?"

"Me and Harley took my dumpstick and went junk-hunting in the weeds down by the West Bridge, and there it was." Harley is Zack's smart little black dog that has blond eyebrows and even wet doesn't smell like dog. "Probably this briefcase slid off the top of some guy's car when he went around the corner to get up on the bridge."

"Yeh," I went, "probably stopped for gas at Fring's Service there and left the suitcase on top of his car, and then *zip*, when he went around the corner there."

"Yeh," went Zack, busy with his little tiny hex wrench. "That's what I just said." His straight red hair is getting long again and falling in his eyes. Zack is also getting sort of smart-mouth with me and I'll have to find a way to take him down a peg or two, but I have to admit he is a pro with his hex wrench. What he does is, he holds the long end with his little pliers. Then he uses the bent end like a key. Zack can get into anything with that outfit, I swear.

"Probably you could see the keyhold better if you wiped off your glasses."

"I am training myself to look like I'm in pain, for legal reasons, so don't worry about the glasses."

Being a student of Criminal Justice as well as International Espionage, I am interested in everybody's tradecraft, so I asked him. "Zack, how come you're using that little hex wrench instead of a paper clip."

"Easy. This Allen wrench is made of steel. A paper clip is made of zinc or something. Anyways, a paper clip bends in your keyway, which makes it useless as a key—except on TV where most stuff is hokey anyways, as you may well know."

Zack always explains stuff to you. Sometimes more than you want to know, sort of like Mr. Keyshot who will give you a whole chapter when you only asked for a verse. The "as you may well know" bit sounds suspiciously like Mr. Keyshot.

But, even though he is two years younger than me and is beginning to talk back, I am tolerant of Zack since he is a senior at Balona High and is pretty smart I give him some cousinly advice: "You probably ought to try to get yourself a lock-pick kit, if you're gonna do this sort of thing for a career."

The lock on the suitcase gives way to the hex wrench, flies open with a *snap*. Zack has unlocked the thing.

"Speaking of which, take a look at that." There, right on top, when Zack had pulled up the lid, there was a lock-pick kit in a plastic case, unsnapped and open so you could see the picks inside. I knew what it was right away from the illustration in my Universal Intelligence Training School catalog. The whole thing was sitting right on top of a bunch of papers and letters. And money. Stacks of it, all wrapped up neat with rubber bands.

"Hey!" I went. "It's money! We're rich." Since I didn't win the Lotto, even though I *thought* I almost did recently, I usually get pretty enthusiastic at the sight of lots of money. And there was plenty in this suitcase. Also, in Balona we usually go by the old sawbones, "Finders keepers, losers weepers." Which means you lose it in Balona, forget it. It's gone.

"And a notebook here, and another notebook, both full of little writing. And underneath here are maps and letters and some sort of official certificates stacked up, see, here under the socks and the toothbrush. Here's some tools, knives and stuff—hmm, nice and razor-sharp—wrapped up in this leather roll. And these are British pounds, as you may well know. Or not know. See, this is the Queen here."

We were sitting on Zack's bed, in Zack's bedroom, upstairs in Zack's house where his mom had gone to some garden show and his ancient dad was asleep as usual in his office down on Front Street.

Zack sucked on his tooth braces, adjusted his white foam neckbrace which he wears often in order to practice his whiplash behavior. "How did you mean, '*we're* rich'?"

"Well, I'm your cousin, a blood relative, and besides, I'm sitting right here, helping you. And I'm older and wiser and an advisor. So you're my mentor. That's how I mean it." I put on my pain look. "You don't mean you're gonna keep it all to yourself."

"No. I mean I'm gonna go over to the *Courier* and put in an ad about it, so I can find the rightful owner." He looked at the stacks of bills. "I wut'n refuse a reward, as you may well know."

Except for the part about the reward, Zack's attitude was distinctly un-Balonan, and I tell him so.

"Well, honk. I am gonna be Chief Justice of the Supreme Court of the United States so, as you may well know, if I don't start doing honest stuff and getting good recommendations, I'll never make it. Mr. Keyshot said so, and so did Pastor Nim."

It's hard to dispossess the advice and words of my blood cousin Nimitz MacArthur Chaud, pastor of Balona's BoMFog Tabernacle, even though Cousin Nim's virtue gets in the way of progress sometimes.

Zack picked up the lockpick kit and turned it in his hand, snapped it shut, put it in his pocket. "Since it's illegal, I wut'n want the poor loser to get arrested about having a lockpick kit, so I'll take it off of his hands, and he won't have to be disquieted." Zack always shows off his vocabulary words. He smacked his lips, the same way his dad, Uncle Kenworth Burnross, does over chicken and dumplings.

"What's that thing, I wonder." I poked at this leather thing that looked like a club.

"That's a baton." Zack tries to give the impression he knows everything. He doesn't, of course.

"A baton is what Bootsie Dwindle throws up in the air and twirls around when the Flag Fems are marching. Everybody knows that. This is not a baton, Young Zack." For some reason Zack doesn't like it when I call him "Young Zack."

"This thing is a baton." Zack went to his huge dictionary and looked up *baton*. There was a picture of the thing in the dictionary. "This guy is maybe a military officer, since he's got a baton. Also, look here. Do you recognize these things?"

There in a corner of the case was a set of the things I have been trying to get for three years now. "Pips!" I hollered. "He's got pips." Harley barked, as excited as me, jumped up on the bed.

"Take it easy, Harley," went Zack. Harley went back to his place on the window seat, looking sort of disappointed.

The gold metal tabs were stuck into a piece of cardboard, ready to pin on your shoulder boards when you put on your uniform for a Queen's Review at Buckingham Palace. Commander's pips, just like the catalog shows.

"And look here." Zack turned over a thick paperback book with a light blue cover. *Manual Number One of the Universal Intelligence Training School—Pronounce it WITS*. "It'n this the same thing you got?"

"Wow! It is the same thing. It's a UITS Manual. This guy is a spy!"

"This guy is *maybe* a spy. Maybe he's just a wannabee. Like somebody I know." Zack was sucking on his toohbraces, a sign that he was being cynical and doubting, and showing how much smarter he is than you. He was also being sort of insulting, but I let that pass, since he is a youth who needs to try out his individuality, and I myself once went through such a phrase.

"Look. This guy's already got his pips. He probably got a badge, too. Probably he's carrying his badge on him, pinned behind his lapel. That's what I would do. I bet he's got a Baretta, too, like James Bond."

"James Bond dut'n carry a Baretta. He carries a Walther PPK." Zack always has to show off how much more he knows about stuff you know.

"I knew that. I was just testing you."

"James Bond is fake."

"Yeh. Well, he's sort of real, if you use your imagination."

"The Walther PPK uses 7.65 ammo. Takes a Brausch silencer."

"Yeh, being practically a pro, I know all that stuff, Young Zack. But this guy is real. Just look at all the evidence: A baton, pips, the Manual, lock-pick kit, foreign money. Probably packing the Walther on him. This guy is for real. You can tell."

"These here are letters to a Silas Blade. So this must be Silas Blade's briefcase." Zack opened a few envelopes and glanced at the contents. "It looks like they're reports about bank accounts and investments and stuff. Dut'n look all that important."

"Let me look, too, will you!" Zack always has to hog the best stuff for himself. He finally let me look at one letter that had no envelope or stamp. "This one's a copy of a letter the guy sent to somebody. It says, look here, it says, 'I never violated your trust, whatever unscrupulous persons may have told you.' And it goes on like that. This guy was having problems with somebody over there, it looks like."

Zack sat up and picked his nose, always a sign that he's thinking. "Well, maybe it would be useful to make copies."

Zack is a spoiled only child with a ma that makes gourmet sandwiches for him and a dad that gives him an allowance. He's got his own TV that he watches TV chef Davy Narsood on and then practices making weird food for himself. He will probably get his own car one of these days, if his dad starts remembering who his kid is instead of forgetting to put on his own pants in the morning. So, anyway, to make a long story short, Zack has a computer and printer and scanner and his own phone line and a copier all lined up along one wall of his room. He started to make copies of all the documents in the briefcase.

"Are you going to copy everything?"

"Only the notebooks and the stuff that looks interesting. Not the dumb manual, since you got one of those, but maybe a pound note or two, just for the novelty of it. It might be useful down the road, except the paper feels different."

"I wonder who the chick is." I was looking at the black and white photo of a glamorous doll in a gold frame.

"Well, it says right there: 'Natasha,' where she signed it with eternal love across her boobs. I think I'll make a copy of the picture, too." Zack didn't even take the picture out of the frame, his copier is so high quality. Spoiled rich kid.

"So," I went, "when do we take the case over to the *Courier*?"

"Well, honk. Right now."

So I accompanied my young cousin and Harley over to the *Courier*, where Zack negotiated with Mr. Patrick Preene about how much it would cost to insert a "found" ad. Zack convinced Mr. Preene to charge nothing at all, since it was a public service,

Zack said, and Mr. Preene agreed finally, after Zack showed him the money inside.

Me and Zack decided maybe we should put a watch on the *Courier* office to see who showed up to claim the case. It occurred to me that maybe the guest we took to our house last night, Commander Burberry, him being another secret agent, might possibly know this guy. Secret agents usually keep to themselves because of security reasons, but sometimes they get together to shoot the breeze over old times. I decided to find Commander Burberry, if he would still talk to me after my ma's behavior last night, and ask him if he knew of a Silas Blade.

# 4

## Billa Crinkle at Kute Kurls & Nails

"He is just the handsomest man I ever saw, is all. He's got the great biggest beaver-brown eyes you ever saw. And tall? He's tall. And he's got a nice sweet breath you can get a sniff at when he leans over and croons at you. Not like nowdays where you get most Balona men smelling like mustard and korndog. This gentleman smells sweet. I tell you, I'm in love!"

Sophie talked back right away: "Billa, you think everything in pants is sweet. What is this, the thirtieth time you been in love? Don't move your head around so. I can't do a thing while you're moving so."

"It's how he looks at you, y'know. He sort of gets inside, behind your eyes, like. Oooh. Makes me shiver."

"Don't shiver while I got this thing near your eye, or it'll poke it right out. Ain't you getting kind of ripe for another love affair?"

"Well, some of us slim types just matures later than you big fat girls. I still got room to grow."

"Uh-huh. Just how old are you now, Billa?"

Silence, except for another chapter of *The Young and the Ruthless* from the wall TV and an oldy by Bob Wills and his Texas Playboys twanging over KDC-FM from the shelf over the sink.

"He come looking for a room, where only last week I finally put the sign in the front window. I guess I'm just lucky. Nice car, except sort of dusty and no hubcaps. 'No suitcase, just that thing?' I went, since he come up to the door without a suitcase or even a paper bag, only a square hunk of wood. Nice and shiny, looked like it was solid wood. 'My case is temporary lost,' he said. "This box contains a few personal items." He held the box (which it actually was a box) under his arm, tight, but I cut'n see where the lid on it was. He was very distinguished sounding, so I ast him in, and we had a cuppa Postum right there in my kitchen."

"You wat'n afraid of getting raped right there on your kitchen table by this strange man you left in with no references?"

"What? He said he come recommended from my little Cousin Kenworth Kuhl. That's maybe not top references since I consider

Kenworth my nothing-cousin, but anyways it's hometown. Anyways, girls, I'm a keen judge of flesh, and this young feller is quality stuff, let me tell you. Got a widow's peak and long thumbs, and you know what that means. When he it'n looking into your eyes, he's got his eyes lowered, like he respects you. Put in plenty blue today, girl."

"Maybe he had a hangover and caused the lowered eyes."

"What? I already told you how sweet he smelt. He said he was English. Sounded like it, too. Elegant. Held his cup up just so, sipped at it. Dit'n lean over and slurp it like a Balona feller would. He also spoke up so a body could hear, not like some folks around here. And he had a sore arm, so I got some liniment and give him a nice rubdown, right there in my kitchen."

"I hope he put down his cup."

"He just come from Bapsie's."

"Well, that'll explain something. What's Bapsie done this time?"

"Well, she was a couple sheets to the wind when Kenworth brought him home to stay the night. Y'know, the courteous thing to do to a stranger in town."

"The courteous thing to do is let him get out of town fast."

"What? Well, she wut'n let him get to bed without she and him had an arm-wrassle, y'know?"

"Bapsie arm-wrassled with the beaver-brown stranger."

"Beaver-brown eyes, yeh. Of course, she just about took the arm out of his socket, so he was some worst for wear when he showed up at my house."

"Well, you fixed him up, I bet."

"I went and give him a nice massage. Fixed him up for sure. No hair on his back at all."

"You got him to take off his shirt?"

"I told you, the man was in pain."

"So after the massage you went and rented out Mr. Keyshot's room?"

"I went and rented it out before the massage. What you think I am? Anyways, I think of Ab's room as a *spare* room. Mr. Keyshot was just a ship passing in the night. Mr. Keyshot's got his own place now. You all know that. Mr. Keyshot had took down Ab's picture. Put it in the closet behind Ab's tux. I resurrected it back up. I also give that wimp what-for with my golf club, y'know. Or maybe it was my softball bat I konked him with."

"Of course, Mr. Keyshot was really Mitzi's ship passing in the night there at your house."

"Well, my daughter has had a few of those, yeh. Mitzi's in Fresno now. I can't get her station on my radio without a lot of static, but she's on every morning and sometimes at night, too."

"You ast her advice about this new gentleman you got living with you?"

"I ast Bena. Mitzi don't have enough sense to give me advice."

"By Bena you mean that real nice old lady Ms Verbena Splinters?"

"Yeh. Bena. Like I said. And Bena's a lot bigger and fatter but she's also some younger'n me, Miss Patella Knows-it-all, so you should put down your pencil and pick up your broom again. And don't go talking about *old* ladies. And she's not so nice, either."

Sophie again: "You dit'n ast any of your girls?"

"What? My other girls beside Mitzi don't give a damn about me one way or the other. Mr. Burberry does."

"That's his name?"

"Simon Burberry. I told you. It'n that distinguished sounding?"

"Sounds like a raincoat or a car polish. Maybe a ice cream flavor."

"What? He went right on into Ab's room and first thing opened the closet, looked around in there. He went, 'I have a few fine wooden boxes to store in here. I'll bring them in from the car, if that's all right with you.' Then he bounced on the bed, said it felt nice. Said the window faced the right direction. Said he come to Balona to get away from the crowd. He don't want people to know he's here, so don't tell everybody everything or write it down and publish it like you usually do, okay, Miss Patella Knows-it-all?"

"I'm just writing down some notes for deep background. Maybe on a column I'll do about you, Mrs. Crinkle."

"Well, don't do no column on Mr. Burberry, on account of he said he dit'n want attention."

"People are always saying that, Mrs. Crinkle. But they really want to see their names in the paper. And their picture, too."

"You can put my picture in the paper, but I will get very upset if you write up Mr. Burberry, that poor man. He needs his rest. Mr.

Burberry give me a hunnert. On account, he said. The boxes he brought into the closet wasn't really small, like he said. They was like the box he had under his arm, about a foot each way. Nice shiny wood, but you cut'n see a lid on any one. Looked like solid. But nice looking boxes. Stacked 'em in the back of the closet, whistling all the time. Sweet whistler. I bet he could get on the TV with his whistling."

"I thought you cut'n hear so good, Billa."

"I can hear whistling like an ace. Mr. Burberry's whistling is low and sweet. Can't remember the name of the tune, but it's sweet, too."

Sophie: "How much you gonna charge him?"

"Depends on how much he eats, since he's boarding, too."

"Well, you just watch out, now you got a man living with you again."

"Hee hee, he's the one better watch out!"

"You better not mention about Mr. Keyshot any more, Billa. Here comes Bellona Shaw."

"Bellona Shaw's a damn foreigner busybody."

"She's been here 17 or 18 years, Billa."

"Damn foreigner busybody."

"Hello, Bellona. What's for you today?"

"Hello, ladies. I'm tired of red. I want to be a blonde."

"You want to be a blonde *again*, you mean. So, okay, have a seat and watch the TV till I get Billa here fixed up. Won't be a sec. Hold still Billa. I want to wipe up here so you don't get that stuff in your eye."

"I've just seen the dreamiest Englishman."

"Oh, on the TV there? Let's have us a look, Sophie. Turn the damn thing around so we can see it over here."

"No, back at the *Courier*. Came in wondering about a lost briefcase, and little Zachary Burnross had just turned it in, dear honest little fellow. We hadn't even worked up the ad yet. But what a fine-looking man. What style!"

"Careful, Bellona, we got Miss Knows-it-all here."

"Oh, hello, Patella. I bet Patella would agree. Fine looking man with steel-gray eyes."

"My fine-looking man's got beaver-brown eyes. English, too."

"Stop moving your head now, Billa, I told you."

"We have two Englishmen in Balona today? Now that's worth writing about, eh, Patella?"

"I don't know, Mrs. Shaw. Mrs. Crinkle here said I shut'n write about Mr. Burberry, since he wants his peace and quiet."

"Hush, Patella. You said Mr. Burberry, Bellona. Simon Burberry? My Simon Burberry with the beaver-brown eyes? Tall, elegant Englishman?"

"No, Billa, I dit'n say 'Simon Burberry.' Patella did. But my Simon Burberry's got steel-gray eyes. Tall, elegant Englishman. He's got steel-gray eyes. Rivet right through you, those eyes. Of course, then he looked down right away, down at the floor, respectfully, the way a man ought to do. The man has style!"

"Well, my Simon Burberry is gonna live with me, and he's got beaver-brown eyes. Besides, if you're gonna get anywheres with that wimp Don Keyshot, you better not pay my Simon Burberry all that much attention. Know what I mean? Stop writing in your notebook, Patella."

"You're all through here, Billa. Blue as can be. Here, take a look."

"Not bad for 75."

"If you're 75, I'm 25."

"Stop that writing, Patella."

"I'm not writing. This is just another way you can use to sharpen your pencil."

"Here you go, Bellona. Get on up here. Blonde, is it?"

"Well, if you'll remember the old saying, they do have more fun."

"I'm the one gonna have the fun. You'll see. Put it on my tab, Sophie."

"Well, take care, Billa. Take care of that beaver-eyed steely Englishman!"

# 5

## Simon Burberry

An absolute relief to have the case in my possession again, even minus a significant item. Most remarkably, the money was still there. All of it.

It was not necessary to provide a great deal of information in order to reclaim my case. I spied it at once when I entered the newspaper office. There it lay, its burgundy glow practically lighting the counter. "Ah! My case! You've found my case."

"Little Zachary Burnross just brought it in. Little fellow just left. You just missed him." This from a female clerk standing at the counter drinking coffee from a plastic cup. The female had bright red hair of a particularly disturbing hue. My knees began to quiver in response. I averted my eyes which were beginning to itch.

I reached for my case, turned it about, almost had my key in the lock. Luckily, Frank of Frank's Soupe de Jour had found my keyring and returned it to me just as I crossed the street to my car last night after meeting the Kuhls.

"Well, now just a dang minute." The publisher or editor — chap with a green eyeshade—held up an admonishing finger. "You got to provide some identification, y'know. Not just anybody can come in here and lay claim to a case nice as this."

"I can do better than lay claim to it, sir. I can produce the key. I can describe the contents in detail."

"Well, fire away. You can do that, the case is yours."

With my hand on the closed case I explained the appearance of the letters and bonds and bills therein. I mentioned only "a manual" and a photograph in a gold frame.

"Yeh, looked familiar, too," the fellow said of Laura's portrait. Obviously he had somehow opened and vetted the case. I shall have to give consideration as to how to fortify the lock so that it is not so easily forced. Perhaps I can somehow use the Chinese Technique.

"The photograph? My fiancée," I admitted modestly. "Probably the most valuable of all my possessions, that photograph!"

"What're those things there?" He was pointing his thumb at the small container containing my eye colors. I should have left them in my disguises box.

"Mm, those are some scientific lenses for my study."

"Oh, yeh? You a scientist, are you?"

"Anthropologist, yes."

"Oh, yeh. Spiders." He shuddered. "Well we got 'em around here all right. Except the best kind, the Black Widow, sort of holes up in the winter, y'know."

"Yes. The Black Widow. I see."

The redhead was frowning into her cup. Perhaps she caught the jest. Perhaps she was puzzled.

"Well, the case is yours all right. So you wanna give a reward for it?" The newspaper chap spoke in the blurred tones I have come to believe may be typical of this river-delta area of north-central California.

"Of course. I would say a hundred dollars should be a fitting sum for an honest young fellow, don't you think?"

"Well, there was a lot of money in there, it seemed to me, from where I looked at it. Just a quick look. But I guess for a foreigner, a hunnert dollars is a lot of dough. Say, you ever think about joining Solidarity?"

"I regret that I am not familiar with the organization, sir."

"Well, it's a group of fine fellers get together for breakfast ever so often, shoot the breeze, do good works. You look like you might be a fine member—emphasis on the fine." He snorted.

"I regret that I am not necessarily to remain a member of this splendid community."

"Oh. Well. Just a thought. You change your mind, you let me know, hear?"

I left two $100 bills with the editor. "I trust this will find its way to the young man, the savior of my case?"

"Sure, of course," he said. He was fat and short, with a large nose. What was left of his hair was red. His brown-eyed glance was shifty and their appearance stimulated my own eyes to intensify their itch. I resolved to remove my contacts as soon as I reached the car.

I was followed to my car by the redheaded woman. "You forgot your keys, Mr. Burberry," she cried, handing me the keyring. I must have inadvertently left them on the counter.

In the car again, I felt happy and relieved that I had again my notebook in hand. I made some notes at once. Will the youth actually be given the money? Perhaps. I must try to become more trusting.

My experience this morning with Ms Crinkle was a most interesting introduction into American small town customs.

I had groaned unintentionally when I sat at her invitation to morning coffee. The coffee was an interesting local brew. Not exactly piquant, but flavourful with plenty of milk and sugar.

"You got a pain?"

"I spent the night at the Kenworth Kuhl residence and had an experience there."

Without my having betrayed my embarrassment, she knew at once of my plight. "You lost to Bapsie Kuhl, dit'n you!"

"I engaged in a sporting contest with a very strong person."

"And lost, dit'n you!"

"I have a very sore shoulder," I admitted.

"You shut'n of did that. Everybody knows Bapsie is the strongest arm-wrassler in Chaud County. She could probably take young Sal Shaw, and he won the Valley Crown, y'know. Bapsie was waiting for some unsuspecting sucker to show up. Bapsie's like that. She'll wait for the opportunity to give you a sucker punch."

"Well, I'd joined her in a drink of—I think you call it Early Times—and one drink led to another, and before you know it, there we were at the kitchen table. A young heavy-set youth—'Richie,' she called him—had a video camera on a tripod, and lights, and the entire unwholesome spectacle was recorded, I'm sure."

"Yeh, well, Bapsie shows us them videos when we're over there playing bridge and eating her horse derves. She's collected a whole bookcase full of them videos. You don't wanna mess with Bapsie Kuhl. Everybody knows that."

"I know it now." I groaned as I raised my coffee cup for the dregs, whereupon Ms Crinkle took me by the elbow to my new bedroom and provided me with a very unexpected and unusual service. She massaged my shoulder so expertly that I fell asleep on my newly rented bed.

The room is not large, but the bedding is clean and fresh, and the bed itself is of great size. It faces a wall upon which hangs a large photograph of a glowering face whose eyes follow one. I considered removing the portrait from the wall, but Ms Crinkle mentioned that the last roomer had done so, and that she, Ms Crinkle, had been deeply offended by that act.

Laura's portrait will achieve a place of honor on my bedside table. Unfortunately, most of that table's surface is taken up by a tasteless lamp whose glowing ceramic base appears to consist of numerous young women entwined in complex lascivious poses. Perhaps the subject matter is perceived by the casual observer merely as unremarkable abstraction because of the bland coloration of the sculpture, but to the trained eye the lamp base comprises unmistakable erotica. There may be more to the elderly Ms. Crinkle than meets the eye.

I wonder how my nubile Laura is feeling. I wonder about her state of mind, and whether she is contemplating another screen rôle in the near future. Of course, given her present circumstances, she is not. Silly me.

The thought of my pitiable arm-wrestling performance being screened during a bridge party gives me pause. But perhaps it is better than publicly broadcast TV news photos of my multi-punctured corpse discovered in a motel on the Interstate.

In reviewing notebook entries, I discovered folds in the paper where none had existed before. It appears my notes may have been compromised. Perhaps it was the editor. Or the obliging key-delivering redhead. Or perhaps the person who recovered my case reviewed my notes. As that person is a local youth, I may be in no great danger of discovery. If my experience of Editor Preene and the Kuhl Family provide any comparison, the brainpower of local Balonans does not appear to challenge mine.

The notes did reveal in some detail my most recent experiences with the Redruth-would-be-Tudwicks. I should not have recorded the fact that Lady Demelza had told me she found me to be "attractive." I should not have recorded the fact that she preferred that I serve occasionally as her personal chauffeur, even though Madog had been hired for that very purpose, and had loads of driver experience over my own.

Of course, Lady Demelza was attractive herself—attractive in the way a quite elderly woman can be stunningly if pointlessly attractive if she works at it: bright red lips and nails, superbly

27

gowned and coifed at all times in an expensive wig, heavily perfumed, distancing herself from close inspection. I should have found some way to refuse her gift of the earring. "Just because you're you," she had said.

I hesitated to wear the thing off-duty, not knowing which ear to screw it on, and being too bashful to ask someone knowledgeable, sexual-orientation-wise. But of course I had to wear it when driving Lady Demelza. I wore it in my left ear so that it was always clearly visible to my employer. She was most fond of my blond wig with matching mustache that I kept in its own box, and that I wore only on our drives together. I could see her smiling admiringly in the rear-view mirror.

Madog, a Welshman and thus disposed to sloth, is a harmless drudge and cinema addict. He did have a habit of giving me occasional dark looks, but such glances might be ascribed to his jealousy of my household station and general go-for-it enthusiasm about household tasks. He might possibly have been envious of my occasional "exploration holidays," always approved in advance by Lady Demelza. He may have been jealous of my woodworking skill. He did ask several times about my boxes.

Madog had said about my driving the Bentley, "Go ahead, sir. Make my day. Only don't ride the clutch." Madog was the sort of chap who took everything at his ease. He must have been a challenge to his superiors in the Royal Navy where he said he had once been in service, a "hitch" as he called it. I never revealed to him that I planned to be summoned one day to that same organization, probably, as a result of my studies, as a Commander.

Lady Demelza's car was a fine vintage Bentley without automatic anything. "A new Bentley is too dear," said Lady Demelza to her current suitor, Mr. Tudwick, an unfashionable but snobbish somewhat younger man. "Pre-owned is better. Less complicated. Also a lot cheaper." One even had to roll the windows by hand. One had also to unlatch the bonnet by hand, instead of pulling a lever in the driver's compartment. Of course, the car was a bit large for the mostly narrow roads of Cornwall.

Perhaps Mr. Tudwick's murderous pique is an outgrowth of his rage at being constantly referred to simply as "Mr. Tudwick," rather than as "Lord Redruth." But it is only proper that the unmarried Lady Demelza alone should enjoy the noble title.

After all, it was Lady Demelza of Redruth, and of course *not* the toad Tudwick, whom the Queen honored for inventing the scramnoglio. The remarkable instrument will enable any Englishman to comprehend even the rudest of Scots speech simply by inserting the device into the ear. The amazing invention has brought two U.K. countries—England and Scotland—closer together again, as the Queen pointed out in her remarks at Lady Demelza's ceremony of investiture, an occasion at which I had the honor of standing close as an invited guest. Mr. Tudwick watched from a distance. Madog and Blight were, of course, not invited.

Lady Demelza's other inventions have been as creatively awe-inspiring. Just before the occurrence, Lady Demelza confided that she was on the verge of perfecting a scramnoglio for Irish speech. Could now *Cymraeg* be far behind!

On that occasion Lady Demelza was kind enough to allow me to try one of her devices. She searched my face for the response as she declaimed from Tennyson, but as I am a native speaker of English, the appliance did nothing to enlighten me.

"Takes all kinds," Lady Demelza muttered. It may be that the decrepitude of age had crept up on her and that, added to the other, her impaired judgment contributed to her loss of that fine brain.

It is meet and right that Mr. Tudwick should not partake of nobility as a result of Lady Demelza's electronic genius. And his rage should not focus on a simple butler. Ex-butler. Mr. Tudwick's observation might better be directed at Blight, whose name I may have mentioned. Blight is the gardener at the Redruth estate. Blight is a good Cornish name, but as a gardener's name may give one pause. He is a native of St. Ives and thus his many peculiarities are tolerated as "local behavior." Blight is an evil-appearing man, small, dark, a person who constantly mutters to himself. Blight is well known to have been for years a fanatical admirer of Lady Demelza. If anyone is to be blamed, it will surely be Blight.

But I should have written none of this in my notebook. Of course, Doctor Schimpf has suggested that I suffer borderline compulsive-obsessive disorder in addition to my other problem, so it was not possible for me to leave any of this detail out of my quotidian account.

As the door to my new bedroom has no lock, I am concerned about the security of my disguises, so must remember to keep the disguise box re-closed with special care after use. Inspecting each wig carefully, I took the chance of also shaking them out, first having wedged the back of a chair under the door knob so that my industry would not be interrupted.

The blond wig that I wear with the sky-blue lenses had been flattened a bit, but the good shaking soon fluffed it up. The red wig worn with the sea-green lenses is still in perfect shape, but its heavy color and waves do more to attract attention than to disguise the wearer. The color is a fairly dull shade, not the bright hue that so upsets me when worn by mature women. Lady Demelza once remarked that in wearing it, I reminded her of a favorite film crooner of the 1930s. I have resolved to wear the red only at home during the morning hours, and have made a notation to that effect.

As for my wigs, my current favorite and the one I wear most frequently, it needs a good wash. But I fear to hang it to dry on the bathroom shower rail out of a concern for discovery, for I share the facility with my hostess. I shall wait until Ms Crinkle leaves the house for one of her "bridge mornings," an occasion she says is scheduled for tomorrow.

I have made a complete search of the Crinkle premises, including the garage, where I discovered not only lawn tools, but a fine workbench, several hammers, a carpenter's saw, a hatchet, an axe, and a sledge hammer.

Ah! And connexions for electrical appliances situated all along the wall; places where I might plug in an electric cooker as well as tools. And a splendid concrete sink, perhaps two feet square and two feet deep with plenty of hot water from the gas-fed geyser that supplies the house. With its long run of pipe, not a very efficient water heating system, but wonderful in its provision of quick hot water for the garage. No machine tools visible. Most of the carpentry equipment appears to have been used but rarely.

I shall explore Balona and environs for appropriate accouterment and the necessarily high-quality wood. I could begin a few projects here, for I do feel that nagging need to be artistic again.

Are the assassins still on my trail? Are they near?

# 6

## Joseph Oliver Kuhl

"How come you're calling me again, Patella?" Patella is always phoning me up for no reason, and then complaining about something. This time it sounds like she wants something.

"It's about that briefcase Zack found. There's something, like, suspicious about it."

"Yeh, yeh." Patella is always looking for something suspicious so she can write a big column about it in the *Courier*. She thinks she's a big journalism student at C4, Chaud County Community College, where she can't even get on the staff of the paper over there. I know this for a fact since Willow Runcible told me.

"Zack mentioned the briefcase belonged, like, to a man named Silas Blade. Can you confirm that?"

Patella always makes herself sound like Blip Wufser and the News, even to the point of speaking with her lips pooched out, like Blip. She probably wishes she had Blip's beard. "Zack was supposed to be confidential about that sort of stuff. Anyways, that's what the papers inside said: Silas Blade. Ess Bee. Like the gold initials on the outside of the briefcase. So?"

"So how come a man named Simon Burberry came and, like, claimed the case?"

"Mr. Burberry did?"

"You know this Mr. Burberry, too? Everybody seems to have met him already." Patella sounds dissed that everybody besides her has already met Mr. Burberry. Of course, she usually sounds dissed.

"Mr. Burberry spent the night at our house. What I mean is, he slept in our guest room. Our basement chamber." My ma was actually almost polite to Mr. Burberry after she had a big row with my dad and threw him out of the house. I guess Dad went back to the office and the office cot for the night. Ma then beat Mr. Burberry elbows down at the kitchen table.

She even got some clean sheets and stuff, took him downstairs, and made up the bed for him. Which chamber is sort of a guest room, you don't count the mud on the floor down there from our

31

gaswell overflow around Christmas. Mr. Burberry was the first one to call it a *chamber*.

"Interesting chamber," Mr. Burberry said when he saw the stacks of stuff down there. There's a ping-pong table, and on it cartons of souvenirs from my ma's high school days, my dad's golf clubs, and the TV with the coat-hanger rabbit ears. Also Richie's hamster cage (never actually used because stubborn Richie gave the hamster a bath, and then insisted on drying it off in the microwave). On the floor is the weight-lifting equipment Uncle Kosh gave me for Christmas. The weights were never actually used, since the first time I hoisted the bar I got a serious twinge in my shoulder blade, and the wound has discouraged me about becoming another Arnold Whatisname.

Mr. Burberry never complained about the free room for the night, but you could hear the bed jangle its springs every time he turned over, which was quite a lot from the sound he made down there. I didn't mention all this to Patella.

She went, "Your family is a friend of this Mr. Burberry?"

"Yeh. We're old acquaintances from his castle over there where he's invited us to stay next time we're over there."

"Where's that?"

"You know. Over there, like I said." I was exaggerating some about the invitation to the castle. Actually, the castle never came up in the conversation. That was mostly about music and cruel women which my dad agreed about and which caused the big argument. And then my ma brought up the arm-wrestling thing.

"Grandpa says he thinks Mr. Burberry would make a fine member of Solidarity. Specially since Mr. Burberry's got a whole trunkful of money and it'n likely to go on welfare. Grandpa's gonna ast Mr. Burberry to be a Solidarity member. Mr. Burberry already said he wat'n staying long in Balona, but now that he's actually living here Grandpa says he's gonna ast him again."

"Yeh, yeh, yeh." Patella's grandpa is Mr. Patrick Preene. She's always telling me what her grandpa says, which isn't much.

"How come you sound so mean, Joey?"

"I'm in the middle of some thoughts, and you always call when I'm like thinking."

"I can hardly hear you with that noise in the background. What's that noise?"

"I'm listening to *The Rite of Spring* by a famous Russian on my CD player. It's my favorite piece of all time."

"It's sure noisy. Hurts my ears all the way through the phone."

"It's classical music, where I'm upping my culture, like."

"You oughta listen to the CD I gave you."

"I listen to that when I'm in a good mood." Patella gave me a CD with nothing but gooey love songs and violins and harps. " Right now I'm thinking about my classes, Patella."

"You're all resolved to pass English 1B this time?"

"I'm thinking about publishing some poems to add to my fame, so then maybe Doctor Fardel will come to her senses about my talent."

"Mm-hm. Well, what else did you, like, find out about Mr. Burberry?"

"Who said I found out anything?"

"Zack said you were gonna, like, find out stuff and report back to Zack."

"Zack reports back to me. What I mean is, Zack is my *Q*, one of my operatives. I don't report to him." Zack is getting too big for his pants. I have to get serious about that problem. I also have to maintain discretion and be careful not to leak to Patella that Mr. Burberry is actually *Commander* Burberry of MI-6.

"Well, whatever. What was it you found out?"

"Mr. Burberry likes Country and Western."

"Country and Western music, you mean?"

"That's what I just said. Mr. Burberry likes it because the singers are always carrying on about pain and suffering and how women won't give you a break when you're trying to think. Stuff like that." I'm trying here to give Patella sort of a hint.

"Ah! Mr. Burberry is, like, excaping from a hopeless love affair. That's a real good hook for a column."

"I never said any such thing. Where'd you get an idear like that? You can't write that. That's making stuff up."

"Well, you probably don't know anything else about him anyways."

"Do, too!"

"Probably not. You're always sort of, like, bragging that you know stuff, but actually you don't know so much about stuff."

33

"Well, I bet you dit'n know that Mr. Burberry is actually a secret agent."

"No, I did not. And you don't, either. Mr. Burberry is just a nice tall handsome man who is lonesome and happened to get stuck in Balona by accident."

"Mr. Burberry is actually a secret agent for MI-6."

"Oh, pooh! He cut'n be. He's just a regular guy, excaping from a forlorn love affair."

"Mr. Burberry is actually Commander Burberry of the British Secret Service, and he's on a secret assignment. That's a fact. You could ast him, you don't believe me." Patella's really got my goat this time. I can feel my red face and my heart beating *ka-thunk-ka-thunk* with irritation. She thinks she knows everything, when in fact she often does know more than me, and then rubs my nose in it. That can get pretty irritating, especially when she rubs it in.

"Well, thanks for the info, Joey."

"What info is that?"

"How'd you like a nice pizza and a milkshake?" These are Patella's most favorite things, especially after any regular meal.

"I just ate a peanut butter sandwich and a Hires, so my appetite is ruined for the day. You're not gonna write about Mr. Burberry."

"You mean Commander Burberry?"

Patella already knows about Commander Burberry's rank. I wonder what else she knows about him. "What else do you know about him?"

"Well, I've never, like, even seen the guy, y'know, so what should I know, except what I hear people saying?"

"So, okay. What I mean is, you don't really know enough to write a column about him."

"That's exactly why I'm gonna go over to Ms Billa Crinkle's place and interview Mr. Burberry. Find out if he's really a secret agent. I'm gonna surprise him. Not phone first. That's a big-city-journalist technique I learned from reading, something which you ought to learn how to do, Joey."

I've told Patella lots of times I don't like to be called *Joey*. "My name is Joseph or Joe, not Joey. Joey sounds like a baby hippo or rhinoceros."

"Oops! There's a big commotion outside on Front Street, people hollering, so I'm gonna hang up now, Joey, and go take a peek. See you around."

Patella hangs up without intruding another word. Just like a woman. My ma does that, too. She will hang up while she's talking in the middle of a sentence, and then accuse the *caller* of doing it when the caller calls back to find out why my ma hung up on her.

It takes me all of five minutes to trot from my house to Front Street, where there is a big crowd gathered around Cod's office. Cod is our constable. The usual beef is with foreigners who drive through Balona without knowing about Cod's signal.

In Delta City or San Francisco or Modesto, you have traffic signals practically at every street corner. In Balona, you got one. It's smack-dab in front of Cod's office, in the middle of the block, where a foreigner would least expect it.

The real sneaky part of it is the part most enjoyed by the Town Council, since they get the hog's share of the profits. What happens is when Cod, sitting in his office window with his control panel, sees a foreign car (any non-Balona car) drive up, Cod goes to work with his thumbs on his electronic controls.

Cod makes sure that even if the light is green when the victim approaches the signal, it's red when he gets there. If the car doesn't stop right away, Cod lumbers out and climbs into his patrol car and gives chase with his Siren going full blast.

What has happened in this case is that the car stopped all right, but not soon enough for Cod, and the foreigner is making a big argument about Freedom of Speech, Freedom of Religion, et cetera. This foreigner is making a speech, being heard by all the customers and clerks that gathered themselves from Mr. D. H. Carp's Groceries and Sundries, Kute Kurls & Nails, Frank's Soupe de Jour, Hannibal Chaud's Funerals, Frings Bowls, and a bunch of other businesses.

Cod's face is all red. He can't get a word in edgewise. The foreigner's got all the words. The foreigner is actually a real foreigner, since he's talking English with an accent—sort of an English accent, but not exactly like Commander Burberry's. This is really something: two English foreigners in Balona in as many days.

Maybe they know each other. Maybe this one is a secret agent, too. I draw closer to get the drift of the argument.

"Ain't you supposed to be in school?" This from Mr. D. H. Carp, who's always intruding into my business, just because I sort of work for him part-time on Saturdays.

"I'm doing some research, Mr. Carp, and was just about to go over to class right now when I got sidetracked by this noise here."

"English fellow protesting our traffic light. Won't do him no good." Mr. Carp should know since he's a member of the Town Council. He leans in on me, whispers up to my ear. "That other Englishman, y'know, I hear he's got a couple trunkfuls of cash. Is that right?"

I hate to admit I don't know something so I say, "Well, he's probably pretty rich, I would say, probably." Mr. Carp nods his head like he's pretty well convinced himself.

Cod finally loses patience. "You rot no gights," wheezes Cod, in his personal-style speech, which translates out to "You got no rights." Everybody in Balona knows what he means anyway.

Cod weighs about 350 pounds, so the foreigner doesn't have a chance to resist when Cod spins him around, clamps some handcuffs on him. The foreigner is soon hustled off to the office (where he'll get a chance to cool off and get ready to pay his fine). The Balonans all clap their approval and the crowd breaks up. Folks go back to work and shopping. This is the way the system is supposed to work. If you don't know that, don't come here, is the way we think.

It is really fun and also inspiring to see the law at work.

# 7

## Simon Burberry

A shot rang out!

But it was only TV shooting on the telly Ms Crinkle has left on night and day. And over the shots, the sound of a door chime.

Against my better judgment, but necessarily because Ms Crinkle was away for the morning, I answered the bell whistling my favorite tune and wearing my navy-blue silk robe with the shirred sleeves. I had just hung my black wig in the bathroom to dry and was wearing the red wig with the sea-green contact lenses. The Manual cautions that it is necessary to both air and rotate the wearing of these things frequently so that they fit well and stay fresh.

"Wow!" said the heavyset young woman looking up through thick lenses, notebook poised.

"Yes?" I am used to admiring glances, especially when wearing the red.

"I'm looking for Mr. Simon Burberry."

I felt a distinct chill, for I realized in the moment that it is possible for Mr. Tudwick to have engaged *female* assassins, a variation I had not previously considered.

"Mr. Burberry is not here at present. He has gone to Los Angeles and thence to Mexico City. He is long gone from here." Perhaps I did not sound convincing, for the young woman was frowning. Balona seems populated with frowning women. Even Mrs. Kuhl kept a frown on her face all during my labored attempts to earn my bed, and she was determined to dominate. "However, I am a distant cousin of Mr. Burberry, and he has entrusted me to receive his messages."

"English."

"I speak English, yes."

"No, I mean you're from England."

"I have been there, yes." This young woman was also determined, but I, too, was determined not to become a victim.

She did not appear to be the kind of hard case one might expect in an assassin. "Are you with the government perhaps, seeking aliens?"

"Ha ha, you believe in that stuff? Oh, you mean aliens, like foreigners. No, I'm from the *Courier* here to interview Mr. Burberry."

I felt my entire musculature relaxing in relief. "Well, come in then, and have a cup of something." I resolved to continue to watch her carefully while having some sport, perhaps at her expense.

"Eeee!" she squealed and pushed her way past me. "I know this house, since I been here interviewing Mrs. Crinkle and her daughter a couple times. The kitchen is back there. I know where she keeps her Postum." The young woman proceeded to put on the kettle and bring out cups, cream, and sugar. "Mrs. Crinkle is at Bapsie Kuhl's this morning, y'know."

I took a seat at the table and watched her industry. "You are not fearful of being alone with a stranger?"

"I been taking martial arts, so I know how to kick ass. Besides, I know who you really must be."

"Oh."

She mixed the coffee and sat, brought out her notebook, opened it, and sat poised to write. "So, are you a secret agent, too?"

I felt my bones chill. Had she actually seen through my carefully prepared disguise? "A secret agent?"

"Well, Mr. Burberry is a secret agent, I heard, so if another English guy comes along in the same town, in the same house, even if he's a distant cousin, you got to, like, figure it's another secret agent." She fixed her gaze on my wig. "Besides, it dut'n fit so good and the color's too, uh, too weird."

I decided to changed the subject, a tactic the Manual claims is appropriate for such dangerous moments. "I don't believe I heard you introduce yourself." I smiled.

"Oh! Oh, gee, yeh. Did I forget to do that? How dumb of me. I'm Patella Euphella Sackworth, reporter for the Balona *Courier*. I'm actually a journalism student at C4—Chaud County Community College—but I do part-time stuff here in town." Patella Euphella's purple-plastic-framed spectacles had slipped down on her nose. She was wearing a purple sweat shirt and purple sweat pants and inflated white athletic shoes. An enameled American Flag was pinned to her bosom. She shifted in her chair and sipped at her coffee. "So I'm Patella and you're actually Commander Burberry, in disguise, right?"

I sighed. "You have penetrated to the heart of the matter, yes."

"Well, who's Simon Blade, then?"

My lips chilled for a moment. This was not the sport I had anticipated. But I recover quickly, so I then responded, "Simon Blade is a pseudonym I use when engaged in international work. You're not writing all this in your little newspaper, are you?"

"Well, it's a real big story for a little newspaper when an international secret agent, like, visits Balona, y'know."

"I must believe it is, but understand that when you publish your story, you are putting my life in further jeopardy." The telly gave forth with more shots. I twitched.

Miss Patella's small pale eyes became noticeably larger. "Oh, yeh? I never thought about something like that. Further jeopardy. Gee."

"Yes, there may be assassins on my trail. That is precisely why I chose to visit Balona for a while: to throw them off the track. And it is why I chose to answer the door this morning in disguise."

"Not much of a disguise, by the way."

"Well, it's one of many. I shall give some consideration to modifying it."

"The eyes are pretty good. Actually real good. But you got, like, too much wave in the hair. Greasy looking. Looks like something out of a 90s rock concert. Also it dut'n go real good with the black mustache."

"I apologize, Miss." I felt myself lowering my head, along with my gaze. And I was again employing the subservient verbal response, an occupation-related habit.

"Well, then. Let's get down to it. You're married or not?"

"You are determined to have me murdered, are you?"

"Well, I figure you can take care of yourself, if you're an actual secret agent. And if you're not, then you probably won't get murdered after all, y'know."

Her argument made sense. I would have to think quickly, a habit I have never cultivated, but one that the Manual advises that one must work on.

"I am single." I felt it necessary to add, "In my line of work, a marriage would be awkward, not to say dangerous."

"Yeh, I have noticed some guys around Balona got scars."

"I meant very dangerous."

Miss Patella Sackworth looked at me keenly. "I hear you been, like, associating with Mrs. Bapsie Kuhl. That could be dangerous."

Miss Patella hit the bullseye with that dart, "It is true that I have suffered some small humilations." I forced a chuckle. "But that will pass. In a very short time you seem to have acquired a good deal of information." Now I looked at the young woman keenly. "Perhaps you have been associating with young Joseph Kuhl."

"Heh heh. Me and Joey go to school together, so sometimes he leaks stuff without actually realizing it. Guys do."

"My career is built on that very fact."

"So, Mr. Burberry, what brings you to Balona?"

"As I have said. I am seeking some peace and quiet."

"Well, I wonder what this other fellow, this other English guy is doing in Balona."

Here was unwelcome news and I could feel within me my organs suddenly twisting. "Another Englishman, you say? Recent?"

"Name of Madog, he says."

I could feel the blood drain from my face. I took a quick sip of my now-cold coffee. My hands began to shake. "Perhaps you could warm my cup?"

"You're looking pale. Is this Mr. Madog somebody you know?"

"How do you know of this fellow?"

"He's in Constable Cod's office right now, being searched and interrogated, eksedra. Cod said he was carrying a Walther PPK."

"My god! A Walther PPK."

"But it was a fake gun, plastic, just like the kind Joey Kuhl showed me in Joey's catalog, where you can, like, buy all kinds of fake spy stuff."

"My word! Fake spy stuff, yes, indeed. I wonder why he was carrying such an instrument." Madog must have rifled through my things left in haste back home.

"I bet he was carrying it maybe because a fake is cheaper than the real thing. Or maybe to frighten people with. Who knows."

"How do you know this, Miss Patella?"

"Just call me Patella, Simon." Patella mixed me another cup. "Well, I went in there as a member of the press and, like, witnessed part of the interrogation, sort of. Mr. Madog isn't very suave. After Cod twisted his arm a little he confessed right away that he was a secret agent on the trail of an Englishman named Silas Blade who is some kind of a criminal. He wut'n say what kind exactly, only that this Silas Blade is a slippery character and dangerous to your health." Ms Patella gave me another keen look, modified by a smudge on one of her lenses. "Are you a criminal, Simon? Or is it Silas?"

"A criminal? What bosh! I am not a killer. I have never killed anything, not even a fly lately. Do I look like a killer, Miss?"

"Patella. Actually, take away the red waves, you look pretty good to me. I said *criminal*. Did I say *killer*? I never said *killer*. You're the one said *killer*. Say, everybody in town knows you're staying here with Billa Crinkle and that you got a trunkful of cash. Everybody's after you to join Solidarity. No protection here at all. You want to move, you could, like, stay at my house. We got a spare bedroom. It's right next to my bathroom that's got a door on each side, one for you and one for me. I could slip you in there without even my ma catching on, since she never goes in there except once a year to air out the drapes."

"What did Madog say about my criminal career?"

"He listed a couple who he said 'suffered horribly.' One of a lady and her boyfriend."

"Any kind of suffering is horrible enough, I'm told. But I wouldn't know from personal experience."

"I thought secret agents made guys suffer all the time, secretly, horribly."

"That's just in the fiction, y'know. Mostly we outfox our adversaries. Report them to the authorities. That sort of thing."

"Sounds pretty dull."

"Mostly bureaucratic. Filing reports. You know."

"Oh. So then, you deny being a famous criminal. It figures. How many famous criminals would confess to a reporter?"

Miss Patella Sackworth is possibly a cut above the average Balonan in the brains department. I lapse into a blue funk. Mr. Tudwick was obviously fabricating his own suffering in order to cast his revenge—revenge for no provable offense whatsoever. I wonder if Madog could have been responsible for the lies about Lady Demelza's presumed infidelities.

"You thinking about your victim list, maybe? Or Madog's? Maybe Madog is the criminal."

"Madog is the chauffeur."

"If Madog is the chauffeur, you must be the butler!" Miss Patella's eyes crinkled, her generous abdomen shook with merriment.

"Yes, that's the English way!" I joined her in humourously derogating the very thought of Burberry as butler.

"Well, if you wasn't a secret agent, after all, what might you actually be?"

"Ah. Well. I shall have to think about that. How about anthropologist?"

"Ah! A foot doctor." She looked me up and down, pursing her lips at the shirred sleeves. "You're a foot doctor? Actually?" The pencil whirled in the notebook.

I changed the subject, after advice from the Manual. "I notice you use a pencil rather than a ballpoint."

"Ballpoints are always running out of ink. With a pencil, all you got to do is, like, get out your knife and.... You sure your real name it'n Silas Blade? Mr. Madog swears it is. He showed Cod a newspaper clipping, and sure enough, there was 'Silas Blade' printed right there."

"And it said Silas Blade was a criminal?"

"Not actually, but the clipping was torn. Just showed a fuzzy picture of a guy with blond hair and light-color eyes with the name 'Silas Blade' under the picture and the word 'wanted' there, too.

Nothing about a criminal that I saw. Photo dit'n actually look a whole lot like you. Just some."

"Well, there you have it. Evidently Madog is part of a plot to disgrace me. Ah! I have it. I should confront him, now that he's in handcuffs and no longer has his PPK."

"The PPK was fake."

"Well, I wouldn't know that, y'know. I could have died from heart failure or a brain seizure."

"We say 'heart or stroke.' Maybe then Cod would arrest you, on the basis of Mr. Madog's testimony. His word against yours. I say you should excape this place and, like, come over to my house. I got my own blender where I can mix you up a nice home-made milkshake."

"I'll have to think on that." And did. I decided not to reveal my presence to Madog. I also decided to continue to take my chances with Ms Crinkle.

# 8

## Joseph O. Kuhl

I am thinking about taking choir or autoshop to fill out my program for this next semester. I am anticipating a back-breaking load of academic classes and need some fluff. With my percussion background I would have no trouble in becoming a star of the choir. Or, having a good car of my own and required to study it, I might finally understand how it works.

Zack says I should take a science class, but I had my fill with high school biology where you have to cut up a frog and a pig. Took me off of my appetite for a week each time. Zack says that reaction was not conspiratorial with my *sang froyd* (German for *Kuhl Blood)*, which should make me immunized over such stuff. Probably my Chaud Blood is weakening my Kuhl Blood, only I would never dare say that to my ma who thinks her Chaud Blood is like champagne, or at least Valley Brew.

Speaking of beverages, I was sitting on the landing during my ma's bridge party, drinking my favorite: a Hires. The landing is my usual perch. Nobody expects me to be there, since everybody expects me to be in class. But, of course, thinking about next semester's class load takes the joy out of going to class this semester, so a guy might just as well stay home and rest.

Since nobody expects me to be sitting there on the carpeted stairs, out of sight but close enough to hear even the chewing and swallowing that goes on, I can also hear all the latest gossip going around. I sometimes take notes on these occasions, since I know shorthand, and it's good practice. The reason I know shorthand is too long-winded to explain here, but with even an incomplete semester of it back at Big Baloney, I can still write it like a champ. (Reading it afterwards does present some problems, though.)

My ma's bridge parties are famous all over Balona, probably all over Chaud County, since all kinds of stuff gets discussed here. What's being discussed today is Mr. Burberry.

"He's a cute little guy," went my ma.

"'Little.' Why he's six foot if he's an inch," went Billa Crinkle, a real old lady and a distant relative, since she's also a Kuhl originally.

"Well, he's littler than me." Which is true if you multiply how tall you are by how much you weigh. My ma has what she calls a "full-figured beauty with bee-stung lips." During her bridge mornings she also wears her "good luck" torn yellow muu-muu with the three-year-old maplenut ice cream stain over one boob.

"And he's weaker than you, I hear," went Aunt Pippa, who is Zack's ma.

Everybody laughed, like it was expected that my ma would be stronger than anybody, which is usually the case.

"Well, he certainly looks like he might be a very strong person. Steely gray eyes and long, powerful-looking fingers." This from Mrs. Bellona Shaw who works for the *Courier* and writes columns on Balona Society, gardens, and pets. And also art. Stuff like that. Mrs. Shaw is sort of a shocking curly blonde today. I didn't recognize her when I saw her out the window. She's usually a redhead.

"We're not gonna go through that again, I hope." Billa Crinkle sounds disgusted. "I told you, his eyes are brown. Beaver brown. Just take my word for it."

No response from Mrs. Shaw, since there's no winning any argument against Billa Crinkle. Or my ma, either, who chimes in. "Yep. Beaver brown eyes. I seen 'em close up, I guarantee you. So just shut yer yap about steely gray, Bellona."

"Well, whatever. You do know, don't you ladies, that he's been accused of being a major criminal of some sort."

Aunt Pippa: "Oh, yes, I heard that yesterday, from Sarah, and she should know since she squeezes poor Cod for every bit of information that poor man might possess." The Sarah that Aunt Pippa was talking about is Constable Cod Gosling's ma, another Kuhl cousin of mine. That means Cod is sort of a cousin, too, only nobody in my family wants to talk about that.

Aunt Pippa went on: "Sarah said Cod dut'n believe that other Englishman who got caught in the traffic light trap. Dut'n believe him for a minute. Said the other Englishman had a sneaky way about him. Anyways, Cod went and checked it out with Anson Chaud's office where they've got a link over to the government there in Washington, y'know."

45

Aunt Pippa means the FBI, which she obviously doesn't know the correct name of.

"And they don't have any America's Most Wanted bulletin out on Mr. Burberry at all. Anson told Cod they were concentrating on bank robbers and terrorists, not some foreigner minding his own binnis who might or might not be a criminal somewheres else. The other Englishman was lying, nobody knows why. Anyways, he's gone now, since Cod nor nobody would tell him where Mr. Burberry might be."

"Well, my big brother knows his binnis. Everybody knows that." My ma's brother is Sheriff Anson Chaud, so he is my Uncle Anson.

"Anyway," went Mrs. Shaw, "whatever his eyes, he surely has style. A certain look about him. I wut'n be surprised if he was royalty in disguise."

"I thought you was hung up on Mr. Keyshot, so what's this with smacking your lips over Mr. Burberry?" My ma always asks important questions.

"I'm not hung up, as you put it, Bapsie, on anyone. I am one who appreciates style, and Mr. Burberry certainly seems to have it. By the way, ladies, Mr. Keyshot has style also."

"Bellona's not prejudice if it wears pants." Everybody laughs at my ma's humor.

"What kind of royalty? Like a king or something?"

"Well, perhaps a duke or a baron or an earl. Or a count. I'm not up on my titles. Sorry." Mrs. Shaw takes a loud slurp of her coffee. "Ow! This coffee is really hot, Bapsie."

"We're famous for hot around here. Complain to Mrs. Earwick, not me. I just eat it. Speaking of which, let's dig in."

Now they all stop to stoke up on horse derves, which my ma's househelper Mrs. Earwick warms up in the microwave every few minutes and brings out to the table. Since there's only one table today, and my ma made a big deal about how she was expecting two tables, there's plenty of horse derves for everybody, which you can hear being chewed up, swished around with coffee, and swallowed—all the while they're talking. If I wasn't full of Hires I probably would be hungry from the sound.

Aunt Pippa speaks up about the feature everybody is looking forward to today. "Hey, Bapsie. Play us your latest tape!" Everybody shouts their approval. I edge forward on my stairstep, hoping to be able to get a peek.

The tape is shorter than most of Ma's athletic tapes. Mr. Burberry starts out showing how suave he is, whistling a tune. He stops whistling pretty soon, since he is wasted in about a minute flat. My ma doesn't even work up a sweat. On the tape she inspects her nails and covers a yawn with her free hand, et cetera, but you can see Mr. Burberry's forehead perspiring and his eyes almost popping out with the effort.

You can also tell my ma likes Mr. Burberry since she pours him three extra-stiff shots of Early Times to ease his after-contest pains.

"Drink up!" she says, holding the glass for him, since he's obviously too worn out even to lift up his beverage. This is all documented on Richie's tape.

"My! You really did it to the poor fellow, Bapsie." Mrs. Shaw doesn't sound approving.

"Well, he was complaining about how in Country and Western songs the women are always weeping and sobbing, so I figured I'd show him how weeping and sobbing can affect menfolk, too." The women all clapped their hands.

"You should run for mayor," goes Aunt Pippa.

"I been thinking about it," goes my ma. "If I did, I'd win hands down." Ma is always confident.

"Maybe Mr. Burberry is a famous politician recovering from a terrible defeat, which is why he wants to be anonymous." Aunt Pippa is still harping on Mr. Burberry.

"Maybe he's got a fatal disease and has came over here to die. He eats like he's starving." Mother Crinkle sounds worried.

"He does look gaunt, sort of artistic. Perhaps he's an artist recovering from a tragic love affair, the way artists often do."

"You got love on the brain, Bellona. You need to get that wimpy Mr. Keyshot to propose." Mrs. Shaw doesn't respond to my ma's suggestion. My ma doesn't cotton to much talk about love. She's always wanted me to marry Balona's rich heiress Claire Preene and bring the family fortune back to the Kuhls where it belongs, but she doesn't like lovey-dovey talk.

Since the entertainment is over, I decide to sneak away from my comfortable post and go see Cod, get the scoop on Mr. Burberry's accuser myself. When I get to Front Street I see a bunch of flags tied onto the street lamps. "What's the flags for?" I ask Mr. Sackworth, the guy sweeping the sidewalk in front of Mr.

D. H. Carp's Groceries and Sundries. He is also Mr. Carp's assistant. He is also Patella's dad.

"It's Presidents Day." He gives me a hard look like I am prize dunce of Balona. "You're supposed to celebrate and buy things."

It occurs that this is the true self-conscious reason I didn't go to class today. It's a school holiday and my self-conscience knew it without me even thinking about it. That means Zack is probably home, too. I decide to go over to Zack's and see if I can't get him to come along on my visit to interrogate Cod.

Zack is busy with his computer on the Internet as I practice tradecraft, sneaking my way into his house so his ma can't see me. Then I remember that his ma, my Aunt Pippa, is busy playing bridge at my house. Harley sniffs "hello." Zack doesn't bother.

I get on the Internet with my computer, too, but usually so much porn gets in the way that I never get to the thing I was going to look up. Ms Birdie Swainsler, our town librarian (and organist at Tabernacle) is always circulating petitions to have porn exercised from the Internet. But I don't know. You can get most porn free as samples, and if you go from one sample to the next, you can sort of forget about signing up where you have to pay to see it. Where else are you going to get something free nowdays? I think Birdie's petition is sort of un-American. Besides, after a while porn gets to be sort of a drag, being all the same stuff over and over again.

So Zack's face has got a frown on it. Even Harley, a polite and usually happy dog, is sort of frowning. "How come you're frowning, Young Zack?"

"You remember that photo Mr. Silas Blade had in his briefcase? The one I made a copy of?"

"I do indeed. Are you smitten by the love bug?" I crinkle my eyes to hint that I'm making a little jest here.

"No. I thought I'd seen her before, so I went over to the New Oliver where they've got that big display in the lobby."

"The old-time movie display, yes."

"And there she was. It gave her name, right there under her picture. Black and white, like the original, as you may well recall. Would you believe it's not 'Natasha,' after all? It's Laura Loopie."

"Is that a fact. Never heard of her, except her name."

"How come you been holding your mouth funny and talking that weird way?"

"What way is that?" I'm trying out my English accent, but Zack is a bit thick and doesn't get it.

"You sound like you got snot in your nose and a headache. And you're twisting your lip and tilting your head funny, too."

"Never mind, Young Zack. I'm just trying something too sophisticated for most country people. Anyways, what's this about Laura Loopie?"

"Well, probably you've seen Laura Loopie on old movies, black and white jobs on the late show."

"Yes, well, Young Zack, I'm often too busy with my studies to watch the late show."

"Well, whatever. So I've looked her up, here on the Internet. Here she is. Guess what?"

"What? Yeh, there she is. So what? I don't like to guess."

"She's English. And right now she's actually a lot older than her picture here. A whole lot older."

"So? It figures she would be English. Mr. Burberry is English. So Mr. Burberry likes older women. He's hanging out at Billa Crinkle's, and she's about older than anybody in Balona except maybe Mrs. Earwick and my Grandpa Daddy Kon. Mr. Burberry likes older women."

"See here: It says 'Famous Redhead Missing.' It says here that Laura Loopie's been missing for almost a year."

"Missing Mr. Burberry?"

"Missing. Not over there in England any more. Gone from her house with her jewels and stuff. Old lady left her dog. Left letters in her mailbox. Left her bottles of medicine. Nobody knows what happened to her."

"I bet Mr. Burberry knows, since what she wrote on her photo tells you a lot about how she feels about him. Right?"

"Well," goes Zack, very logically, "maybe we ought to ast him."

# 9

## Simon Burberry

Even with assassins potentially lurking in the background, this place does feel like home, what with the fog and now the rain. I have scouted the countryside around and about, and I find that Balona will serve nicely as my *pied-à-terre*. A huge warehouse store at a nearby village known as Fruitstand yielded surprisingly high-quality seasoned hardwood. The same establishment offered two versions of several machine tools, amateur and expert. I chose the expert line. It is such a pleasure having plenty of money!

My own heirloom hand tools will do for the finish work, and I have now acquired a fine circular saw for the rough work, a variety of saws and planes for the finer crafting, and some excellent sandpapers, veneers, glues, lacquers and plastics of surprising good quality, brushes, the necessary supply of binbags, and so on. I also bought a machine with which to Hoover the garage frequently, so as to suppress and collect any vagrant dust that might otherwise soil the surface of my creations while drying. My new boxes should appear to be masterworks of craftsmanship. Some of the boxes that I have stored in my closet must be repaired. Although tightly contained in larger cardboard cartons during transport, they did suffer some scuffing by airline handlers. I must get to work at once.

I am still recovering from the visit I had this afternoon from young Joseph Kuhl and his cousin. Wearing my black-with-brown (my usual Balona-exterior disguise), I was unloading my newly purchased goods from the car, and the two youths appeared suddenly behind me, giving me a such a good start that I dropped several items.

"We shut'n of crept up on the guy like that," said the fat little boy who has the most alarming resemblance to my own fat little cousin Ethelbert, red hair hanging over the eyes, tooth-bands, gold-rimmed spectacles, and all. Of course Ethelbert is 30 years older than this one, his hair is almost gone, and much of his fat has now slipped toward the Channel.

"This here is Zack, Commander. He's only a high school kid, but he does have a smart dog." The dog does indeed appear to be a clever beast. But as I cannot trust dogs not to bite or soil me in some way, I kicked at it when it tried to sniff my privates. It then made a low disapproving sound, not exactly a growl.

"Harley dut'n usually do that to people, Mr. Burberry. So I'm sorry, but you must have an interesting smell or something," said Zack, adding, "My name is actually Zachary Taylor Burnross, future jurist, but Joe here calls me Zack since he probably can't remember my real name."

The two began picking up some of the items I dropped, a courteous gesture given the wet condition of the street and the general environment.

"Hey, you're a carpenter," said Joseph, poking his nose into my cartons and shopping bags and exclaiming loudly at each discovery.

"Hey, you're nosy," said Zachary in Joseph's ear and also frowning at his cousin, an expression that I immediately found reassuring.

"Actually, I'm a wood craftsman, an artist as may have been said, for I create Chinese boxes."

"What's a Chinese box?"

"A Chinese box is not actually a Chinese box, as Commander Burberry may well know. A Chinese box is actually a Japanese box, a little wood box for jewels that's got designs on it and stuff." Zachary closes his eyes when he completes his sentence, as if he has just delivered an important announcement. He also smacks his lips, probably a habit picked up from an elder. I notice such things as part of my continuous practice of tradecraft.

"Zachary is substantially correct, except for the fact that my boxes are not 'little boxes,' but rather somewhat larger ones. And they are puzzle boxes as well. My word, Zachary. How did you know such a thing, about Chinese boxes not being authentic Chinese creations at all?"

"I am a scholar, as Joe here may well know. But I am also a wood craftsman of sorts. And I am also an excellent craftsman in metal, plastic and even, sometimes, ice. And also a great chef."

"He is, too, Commander. I've seen stuff he's made. He's got his own tools. And his food is pretty tasty for only a high school kid." I didn't mention that the food Zack cooks up is a whole lot better than my ma's, and is— usually—free.

"You don't need to refer to me as 'Commander' in public, Joseph."

"Oh. Well, Zack it'n public, so I thought, oh well. Okay." As Joseph appeared crestfallen at my correction, I attempted to remedy that sentiment. "Could you assist me in carrying these things to the garage? That is where I will be performing my art."

"Zack come with me today because he wanted to thank you for the reward. Y'know, the reward you give him for returning your briefcase."

"Of course! Zachary is the Honest Abe of Balona."

Zachary closed his eyes and smirked. "Yeh, I wanted to thank you for the hunnert dollar bill."

"Zack's still got the bill, folded up down there in his shoe."

"The hundred dollar *bill*. I see. Yes. Well, you are very welcome. It was a splendid thing you did to return my case."

"You said 'Honest Abe.' You know about Honest Abe all the way over there in England, Mr. Burberry?"

"Certainly, Joseph. Honest Abe is known world-wide, I would venture to say. Does the dog need to accompany us for some special reason?"

"Well, honk. I wut'n want Harley to get all wet sitting out here in the fog and rain. He won't bite you or pee on your leg."

I allowed the beast to enter with us. It sat near the doorway, watching our every move. It is a small shorthaired black dog with blond eyebrows that move. The young men and I chatted amiably while the dog seemed to listen to our idle social conversation. Its head turned toward each speaker as we spoke, as if it understood our speech. Occasionally it nodded, sagely nodded, it seemed. Unnerving. I may have to take a capsule.

The youths handed me their burdens and watched me set and then rearrange my goods on the workbench, matching the edges of the smaller objects with the larger ones beneath. I will not allow a mismatch to disturb the balance of the composition. I plugged in my portable hob.

"Hey, look at that, Zack. He's even got a hotplate. Hey, Mr. Burberry, when Mrs. Crinkle throws you out, you can come on out here to the garage and fry up a couple korndogs for yourself."

I smiled, perhaps somewhat grimly, recalling the relish with which Joseph's mother threw Joseph's father down the front steps of the Kuhl home. Now Zachary was observing me closely, his eyes suspicious slits. He suddenly asked a question, the seeming irrelevance of which I found odd.

"Who's your favorite movie star, Mr. Burberry?"

I removed my trenchcoat and ascot, hung them on a convenient nail. I must find the appropriate hardware to install in place of the nail. I made a quick note to that effect, a move giving me some time to consider an appropriate response. I mumbled while writing, "Why do you ask, Zachary?"

"I like movie stars and I like to know who likes who, is why."

"Zack also makes movies with his expensive video camera. Better than my little brother Richie any day. Better than most high school kids, probably."

It is becoming obvious that Joseph admires his cousin while being generally irritated by him. I am satisfied with Zachary's response and so explain: "I pay little attention to the cinema today, but when I was a youth I grooved on the American actress Annette Funicello."

"You grooved? He *grooved*, Zack. On who? Never heard of Annette Funicello. She was a teenager?" This from Joseph.

"Well, she was an actress in a lot of beach-type American films. I imagine that she might have been beyond her teens even whilst I was admiring her."

"I guess you like 'em older." Zachary still riveted me through red hair with his smudged-lens look. "I like 'em older, too. I mean, I sort of had drinks with Fionnula Finnegan last summer. She's a famous TV and movie star, y'know."

"That's the truth, Commander. She is. About the drinks, we're still trying to confirm that, since Zack likes to exaggerate his triumphs some."

"Well, honk, Joe! I don't exaggerate my triumphs. Just ast Patella. She was practically there, too, except she left too early to witness the triumph. Patella was jealous, said to me that Fionnula Finnegan was the oldest redhead she'd ever seen."

"She sure dut'n look old on the TV, though."

"I still like Annette Funicello, after all these years."

53

"Well, I like Fionnula Finnegan, whatever Patella says. And I like Laura Loopie, too, for example."

My heart froze in my chest at the sound of the name. But I recover quickly. "Laura Loopie was indeed an older one." I showed my teeth.

"You seen her pictures?"

"Oh, yes. All of them. She's my favorite of all times. In fact, more favored even than Annette Funicello."

"She's *one* of my favorites, Laura Loopie is. I'd like to meet her some day, even though she's old enough to be my great-grandma. You ever meet her?"

"Oh, yes, in my travels I believe I must have come across her at one time or other." It suddenly occurred to me that Laura's photo had been in my case and, if this young man had somehow found a way to open the case, he would be wondering about my story now. I smiled warmly, stroked my mustache, crinkled my eyes in a friendly way. "I should confess that I am actually, to this day, smitten with Laura Loopie and that we, she and I, are in fact the best of friends as a result of my being one of her most ardent fans. We correspond regularly, have pet names for one another. She has even inscribed her photograph for me."

Zachary looked disappointed. "Yeh, well, I just thought I'd ast, since she's such good looker."

"Yes, indeed. She is a splendid looker. I see her often. I find her appearance inspiring. Or I should say I *used* to see her rather often."

"You mean inspiring, considering her age."

"Yes. Her age. Yes, considering her condition, et cetera. Yes." It seemed to me that I was talking too much. Such volubility is not a good thing, the Manual says. I resolved to shut my mouth or change the subject.

"I only seen her in black and white flicks, but the publicity says something about 'The Redhead from Redruth.'"

"Yes, at one time she was a Cornish lass with curly red hair, very red. Very disturbing red. Actually a red wig, I discovered upon meeting her. A great surprise." I could feel the pulse throbbing in my neck, and so turned to use a file on one of Mr. Ab Crinkle's hatchets, first securing it in the benchtop vise. After a few vigorous swipes with the file, the blade began to show silver, sign that a sharp new edge was forming. Quite a stimulating sight.

"You sure got a heavy hand with that file, Mr. Burberry."

Zachary was noticing my disturbance. I needed to distract both youths. "I am envisioning my first box to be crafted in this State of California. I shall name it The Balona Box. Do you know, each of my boxes is unique—ah! not only in appearance, but also in design and, of course, contents. Also, the 'puzzle' of each box is different from the puzzle of any other of my boxes."

"What does he mean by puzzle?" Joseph asked his cousin, not me.

"Allow me to explain, Zachary." And so I did, telling the youths more than they needed to know of the design of my puzzle boxes, how the slats needed to be cut so meticulously and finished so accurately as to move freely, but still keep the nature of their keys secret. "I have had my boxes tested by experts, and none yet has been able to open even one without my personal intervention!"

"Oh, it's like one of them cubes with different colors. What I mean is, one of those things that you got to move around and that you can never get together again in the same way twice."

Evidently, Joseph's experiences with cube devices have been unsuccessful. I trust they shall remain so. The two youths watched my preparations for a while, and then they grew bored and took their leave, the dog following after giving me a long, inquiring look.

I spent the remainder of the day cutting and trimming, humming as I worked, stopping only once to change the overhead light bulb to one of higher wattage so as to increase the level of light at the workbench.

Ms Crinkle yoo-hoo'd for me to come to supper, and I again enjoyed the marvelous korndogs. "It's the National Dish of Balona," she cried.

I enthused about not only the korndog itself—a bit gummy, but flavoursome, tender, and hot from the microwave—but also about the dipping sauce. "What in the world is this wonderful concoction, Ms Crinkle?"

"Well, it's a secret sauce that nobody will ever reveal you, except now that you're in Balona, you might as well know, since everybody else here already knows. It's ketchup mixed up with peanut butter and mustard. The peanut butter is what darkens it up like that, though I'm always careful to use plenty of mustard, too, so it don't look quite so bloody. Everybody who knows anything calls it *Billa's Korndog Sauce*. Ab wanted to go into binnis with it, but he died. That's his photo on the wall of your bedroom, y'know. Strange man. Strange even for Balona."

"Well, I have known some who were doubtless stranger, Ms Crinkle."

"Say, Mr. Burberry, honey, it's about time you was calling me Billa, y'know. I mean, we been associating, y'know."

"Oh. I find first names discomfitingly forward. But one could use the familiar—but respectful—*Mother* Crinkle.

Mother Crinkle made a *mouc*, shook her head, shrugged her shoulders. "Suit yerself."

"But the korndogs are positively delicious, especially with your fine special sauce, Mother Crinkle." Truly better than bangers and mash. I find I could live on korndogs. That might prove to be likely, as Mother Crinkle has served them at every meal.

# 10
### Joseph O. Kuhl

"I wut'n say it in public, but I think maybe the guy's close to being a mental case." This from Zack who wouldn't know a mental case from a pizza, even though he's admitted to having had "psychiatric help" and hangs out with Mr. Keyshot. We were back at Zack's place giving our interview a critique, which is what you have to do if you are in Criminal Justice and you have just interviewed a suspect. Zack is not in Criminal Justice, but I use him to bounce ideas off of.

"What leads you to that conclusion, Young Zack? Your personal experience with loonies?"

"Well, Young Joe, it's he's building those dang boxes. Now, what kind of a international spy builds puzzle boxes like that? I mean, honk, those boxes are too big. You'd have to be a billionaire to use one of those boxes for your jewels. And another thing, he dut'n like Harley. Now, what kind of a normal guy wut'n like a dog like Harley?" Harley nodded his head in agreement, raised his eyebrows and looked at me like he was waiting for a reasonable answer.

I overlooked Zack's insubordination remark about *Young Joe*. "Hey, Zack, lots of guys don't like dogs. My dad dit'n like dogs because of their fleas until Killer came into his life. Now he enjoys the fleas and Killer both. Mr. Carp can't stand dogs, since they doo all over his sidewalk and Mr. Sackworth has to wash it off every morning. Pat Preene dut'n like dogs. He's always shooing dogs away from peeing on the front door glass of the *Courier* building which they do often, since I guess they like to watch their reflection while peeing, like any normal guy. Junior Trilbend dut'n like dogs since he got bit by that dog he stole.

"But those guys aren't crazy, only maybe bent a little, a couple of 'em. What I mean is, just because you don't like dogs is no reason to say you're crazy." Harley wagged his head, frowned with his eyebrows, looked generally disappointed in my answer. I felt for a minute like Doctor Fardel had just rejected one of my poems.

Zack sort of ignored my argument. Just kept on looking out of the window and picking his nose. "You said he said he was driving an Aston-Martin."

"Yeh. Fine James Bond car."

"It's a Ford."

"No, no, it's an Aston-Martin. He confirmed the fact."

"No, it's a Ford without hubcaps and with all the decals and metal Ford gizmos pulled off. It's also got a little rental-car sticker in the back window. Take another look at it. As you will soon well know, it is not an Aston-Martin." Zack opened up a magazine and poked his finger at a Ford ad which showed big city guys smiling at Commander Burberry's car, except this one was green and with hubcaps and without the dust on it.

"Well, suppose you're right. So what? He was just pulling tradecraft. Telling a cover story, like."

"The guy looking for him."

"What about him? He's another secret agent from a foreign land out to smear Commander Burberry's reputation."

"I wonder how come they dit'n send a regular cop if Burberry did a crime. I wonder how come they don't have him on the Most Wanted list. I wonder who all's looking for him—and what for. This whole thing is weird."

"A lot of guys think he's maybe some kind of royal dude who got tired of all the attention from the press and crept off to Balona to get away."

"Who thinks that?"

"Well, some guys I know."

"Who?" Zack can be real irritating.

"Well, Mrs. Shaw, for one."

"What kind of royal dude she think he is?"

"Well, I can't remember all the names she used. Or he could be excaping a tragic love affair. That sort of thing."

"Mrs. Shaw thinks that."

"Yeh. Well, Patella does, and probably other guys, too."

"You know what I think?"

"Usually."

"Well, okay, if you don't want to know."

Now he's got me, since Zack often does have some good ideas, only you never want to agree too soon or he will never let you live it down. "Well, I wut'n mind hearing a theory or two."

"I don't think he's a secret agent at all. I think he's a waiter."

"A *waiter*? Like in a restaurant waiter?"

"Exactly. From the way he stands, like with a towel over his arm, waiting for your order. Look at the way he stands. Like he was a waiter at the Stilton over in Delta City."

Commander Burberry does stand that way. A little. Without a towel, of course. I think about whether I ought to agree with Zack, which is never a good idea to do it right away or he will never let you live it down. "Well, I don't know about that."

"What it'n there to know about that? Close your eyes a minute and see him in your mind's eye. See him standing there. Dut'n he stand like a waiter? Dut'n he look like a waiter? When he was arranging his tools there, he took off his raincoat but he dit'n take off his inside dress coat or roll up his sleeves, not even when he put on his new brown shop apron. Looked like he was about to pour your Hires for you. Your Commander Burberry is a waiter, come to this country to look for work. Or maybe get on welfare or looking for advice about how to get on welfare. A Welfare King, there's your royalty. That's who he is." Zack closes his eyes and smacks his lips. "Dut'n like dogs." Zack muttered that last part.

"I heard that. Wat'n it you who dit'n like dogs last year?"

"That was before Harley."

"Maybe you could get Commander Burberry a nice dog. Convert him, like."

"It's a thought. I don't think I'll call him 'commander,' though. Maybe I'll just snap my fingers." Zack twinkled his eyes, like he'd just made a big joke.

"I don't get it. Say, how come you're limping?" Zack was favoring his right foot.

"I folded my C-note too tight."

"Why don't you unfold it?"

"Think about it. How often does a guy have a C-note in his shoe? I get pleasure from just thinking about a C-note being folded-up down there giving me a cramp."

"You're limping."

"That's simply the price of the pleasure." Zack sounds like my Cousin Nimitz in the middle of a sermon over at Tabernacle. "I wonder whatever became of the English guy."

"The other English guy."

"Of course, the other English guy. The one accused Burberry, said Burberry's name was really Blade. Silas Blade. Sounds to me like that could be a sinister manifestation. I think I'll spend some time studying the guy's notebook." Zack pulls a bunch of papers out of a file drawer. He has made copies of all the pages of Commander Burberry's notebook. Now he starts to sort through the papers.

*Sinister manifestation.* Sounds like a disease. Zack is always using his new vocabulary words, reminding me I've got to study some, too. I think about *Welfare King.* "What about all the money in his briefcase? What Welfare King you ever heard of has got a huge stash of cash like that?"

"Hmm? Well, that's what Welfare Kings get if they're good at it. I'm reading here, so twiddle your thumbs while I analyze these entries." I would take Zack down a peg or two if I knew how.

We sit there doing nothing for a while, me trying to find porn on the Internet, and Zack reading and *hmm-ing* and once in a while *a-hah-ing* through the commander's notebook copy. "Hey, Zack. How come you can't get porn on your Mac?"

"Mummy put a filter on it, she said. She dut'n want me corrupted, she said. She dut'n know I was already good and corrupted by the sixth grade. So she had Sal Shaw come over and do it. No problem, though. I know how to take the filter off any time I want, but I got better things to do. He's got some kind of disease."

Zack will change subjects on you like a flash, so you have to actually listen to what he's saying. With most guys you don't have to worry about that. Most guys will keep saying the same thing over and over, and eventually you'll figure out their meaning. With Zack, *zing*, there comes something he wasn't saying a minute ago. Now it's a disease. "What disease?"

"He's writing here about how Doctor Schimpf wants to cure him, but if he gets cured, he'll miss out on all the fun he's been having doing what he's been doing."

"What's he been doing?"

"Dut'n say. Just about the fun part. He goes on about the capsules."

"What capsules?"

"I don't know what capsules. He just says about them is all. Must be capsules he got from Doctor Schimpf for his disease."

"What disease is that?"

"Dut'n say. Just about the capsules part. He goes on here about the trembling. He trembles. Aha, maybe that's the disease! No, cut'n be. Whoever heard of a guy having fun *trembling!*"

"Well, there must be some disease if he says so, and if he's taking capsules. What else does he say."

"Oh, it dut'n look important. Looks like he copied it out of a book. Here, I'll read it out loud:

*Question: Does beheading hurt? And, if so, for how long is the severed head aware of its plight? Answer: Yes, beheading hurts. How much depends on the executioner's skill, or lack of it. When Mary, Queen of Scots, was executed at Fotheringay Castle in 1587, a clumsy headsman gave her three strokes without quite managing to sever her head. The headsman then had to saw though the skin and gristle with his sheath knife before the job could be regarded as complete. The profound, protracted groan Mary gave when the axe first hit left the horrified witnesses in no doubt that her pain was excruciating. How long is the interval of consciousness after the head is severed? In France, in the days of the guillotine, some of the condemned were asked to blink their eyes if they were still conscious after the knife fell. Reportedly, their heads blinked for up to 30 seconds after decapitation. How much of this was voluntary and how much due to reflex nerve action is speculation. Most nations with science sophisticated enough to determine this question have long since abandoned decapitation as a legal tool."*

"Wow! I never though about that. Thirty seconds. Maybe their head is laying there wondering what happens next, huh! This subject is manifestly sinister."

"Well, Joe, maybe we ought to wonder how come your great friend is copying this stuff into his notebook."

"Commander Burberry is not my great friend, Young Zack. However, he is maybe going to be a colleague of mine."

"However, he is maybe going to be a bank robber. Think about all those bills. Or a burglar. Think about the lockpick kit. Or, or, or a murderer. Think about the blinking heads."

I get a distinct chill to the bladder thinking about these various possibilities. I recover quickly. "However, I hear that the commander is going to be invited to join Solidarity. Those guys will reform him, straighten him out, I'm sure. Just look what they did for my dad."

# 11

## Simon Burberry

My condition has reappeared and I have again resorted to taking Doctor Schimpf's green capsules to mitigate the trembling. I have enough left for only a week or so. The medication still appears to be effective although the terrifying fantasies occasionally intrude, even during waking hours. And of course the capsules tend to promote stomach gas and thus stimulate belching and an execrable taste in the mouth. I am forced to consume peppermints whenever I am in the company of other humans. No further sight, sound, or word of the assassins.

After three days of careful work, I had completed the final coats of plastic lacquer on my first California Box—my *Balona Box*— and it was completely dry, although the weather continues to be wet and the humidity high. I intended to present the box to Mother Crinkle and so brought it to her. I set it before her on the kitchen table.

"My stars. It's beautiful, but what in the world is it?"

I had the response prepared and delivered it in a pleasant voice. "It's a hatbox, Mother Crinkle, for one of your favorite hats." I must say, the box was very well done, one of my very best efforts. Against the chill of the foggy morning I felt the warmth of a prideful internal glow.

"It's not big enough for a hat with any kind of a brim. A hatbox's got to be wider. This looks like a soccerball box. And where's the lid? I don't see no lid? Even a soccerball box's got to have a lid."

Her criticisms were rather strident, if accurate, and I lost much of my glow at once, but my artistry would surely impress her. "Ah! See here how I slide this piece this way, turn the box thus, slide this piece and this one, and *voilà!*" Upon my manipulations the box had popped open, and Mother Crinkle gasped, perhaps in delight, at least in surprise. "A nice space for a fine small brimless hat, don't you think? A hat that at one time was known as a *pillbox*, if I'm not mistaken? Or, of course, if one eschewed hat storage, one could use such a fine box for any number of delicate storage purposes."

"Well, my stars, look at that! But what's that plastic sack in there for?"

"The binbag? Mm, well, to keep the contents from leaking, of course. I mean, to keep it from being leaked into. Let us say you have your fine hat in there and the roof leaks, y'know, and your fine lovely brimless hat could otherwise be ruined." *That's using the old bonce,* I told myself, trying not to grin.

"Well, all my hats got brims, but I don't wear a hat most times nowadays anyways, since I get my hair done over to Kute Kurls & Nails. Wearing a hat on a new hair-do just screws up the hair-do which I pay 20 bucks for. And Sophie's always sucking around for a tip. Not likely she'll ever rate a tip, the job she does. When Ab was alive, it cost me only $3.50. Damn liberals and their inflatulations."

"I would say your blue hair-do is fantastic." I was not exaggerating. The remark was wholly accurate, if not exactly complimentary, but now the lady glowed.

"I'm thinking of becoming a redhead," Mother Crinkle mentioned.

"Oh, I would not do that. Red as a mature woman's hair color upsets me strangely. Can't explain how. My hands start to shake and I have fantastic thoughts. No, I would not advise red for you. Not at all. Not for a while anyway. I mean, red wouldn't go with your skin coloration, y'know."

Mother Crinkle is evidently flattered that I have noticed her skin coloration.

"I'll take you over and introduce you to my friend Bena. She's lately became a redhead. Dut'n look good at all, especially at her age. Probably her huge size and her skin coloration. Maybe you could convince her the way you convinced me." She frowns. "You got a closetful of them boxes now. One stacked over the other. How come so many?"

"I believe there must be a good many hats in Balona that need boxes. When I start on a project, I do not dare to not finish it. I have only in recent years commenced on hatbox-making, dear lady."

"I dit'n mean not to be happy about your present here. Actually, it's pretty nice. Shiny. It'll pick up fingerprints like crazy, though." She sniffed. Possibly the sniffing is a habit with this woman. Irritating habit. She sniffed again.

I could feel a vague hint of trembling coming on. "Yes, one need wipe it clean of prints after handling it. That's true. I wipe all my boxes clean of prints. Habit, I suppose. But that's true of any piece of art, isn't it, dear lady!"

"Hey, that's the third time. You think I'm a dear lady?"

"It's a courteous figure of speech. But, yes, I do consider you a dear friend already. After all, you have taken me, a stranger, into your home. You've treated me rather royally, I must say, korndogs every meal."

"You like them things, what is obvious from the way you dig in. And you like my special sauce. So I figger you like 'em, you get 'em."

"They are baked right here in Balona, I understand."

"Oh, yeh. Right down on Eighth Avenue. Successful binnis, y'know. Eighth Avenue's so heavy used by all them korndog trucks that it's down to mostly gravel nowdays. Needs fixing, all right. Y'know korndogs is not only baked down there, but slaughtered, chopped up, ground, cooked, and stuffed, eksedra. Huge big plant, the King Korndog Kastle Keep where lots of Balona folk work. Looks like a foreign fort made out of stones. Fake stones.

"You stick your head outside about six at night, you can smell when the ovens open up. Of course, lots of Balona folk work at the Turkey Factory, too, but that place smells different let me tell you. When the delta breezes start blowing in the spring, you'll get plenty good whiffs of that place, sorry to say."

"I'd like very much to see the korndog plant in operation. Is that ever possible?" I was thinking of my childhood experience of frequent covert visits to Mr. Prothero's knacker's yard and sausage factory near home, watching that expert at his work. At first the odors were offensive, but the thrill of studying such an artist exercising his talents eventually overcame all reservation.

"Visit the korndog plant? Sure thing. Card Splinters, one of the sons of my friend Bena, was the chopper hopper operator over there for years, 'til he disappeared. They put on a graveyard shift when they get rushed, y'know, and that's when they called in

Card. Sort of part time, because of his condition. So anyways, Bena's sort of a celebrity over there. They call her 'one of our survivors'! Actually got a pass so she can go in and get a free box of frozen korndogs any time she wants. Matter of fact, I get most of my korndogs from Bena. She can't eat all she gets over there, so she passes 'em on to me. Taste the same as store-bought."

"Yes, yum!"

"Well, I'll just introduce you to Bena and I bet she'll take you on a tour. I'll call her soon as I put this thing on the mantel, and we can go over there right this afternoon."

Mother Crinkle carried my box in her apron, careful not to soil the finish with her fingerprints, placed the work of art next to the bronze urn containing, she has claimed, the ashes of her latest husband.

"Got nothing in it, I guess."

"Well, not yet."

"Hm, Ab's a little too tall to put inside the box, but maybe I could put him up on top of it." Mother Crinkle tried several arrangements. "No, too high. Looks like he might topple right off. I'll just leave him next door to your box."

"Dear lady, it is *your* box and, I must say, the juxtaposition of the two objects is quite fetching artistically." I felt an urgent need to adjust her placement, and did, matching the two objects edge for edge, whistling quietly, thinking productively as I adjusted.

We had korndogs and red cabbage for lunch and, Mother Crinkle's having secured the invitation from her friend, we drove to the Splinters residence in a fine gentle rain.

I must confess to having been less than suave in my first contact with Mother Crinkle's tall stout aged friend, for in addition to the purple muumuu, the lady was wearing a long, curly wig of that very tint last donned by Lady Demelza. My pulse began to race at once, and it was all I could do to keep my hands at my sides and my head bowed respectfully.

"This here is Bena, Mr. Burberry. She's been my friend for I don't know how many years. It sure smells funny in here, Bena. Bena's first husband was school superintendent way back when, and her recenter husband was sheriff, dead now for how long, Bena?"

"Stan's been gone 22 years now. Good man. Not as smart as my first husband, but a lot better provider, that first one having been a school person, not well paid at all. Used to criticize my size and my use of the language. I used to tell him, ast for that raise, you dummox, but he wut'n. He'd only say he was grateful to be working at a job where he could do some good, and I'd tell him he was a idiot, that he could do as good at the St. Vincent de Paul, for no pay at all. I will say them Balona schools have went downhill since then. But then Stan come along and winked an eye at me and....well, you know, Stan had something...." Ms Splinters went on in this vein for some time, Mother Crinkle often nodding her head and contributing clarifying information.

Ms Splinters came to an abrupt halt, gazed at us as if in alarm. "How come you folks're over here?"

"Bena, I told you already twice. Mr. Burberry here is a korndog fan. And he wants to see the plant. I told him you could get him in over there."

"He wants to work over there? Why'd he want to do that?"

"I dunno. Probably he wants to take a look is all."

"It's a pretty smelly place. I keep telling 'em to clean up over there, but they only take a hose and squirt off the front of the Kastle Keep. They say nobody ever goes in the back part there. They always serve coffee and korndogs to the inspectors what come around ever couple years or so. So what's the profit keeping the whole place hosed down all the time? Say, I gotta take this damn thing off. It's itching me something awful." Ms Splinters leaves the room in great haste and returns as quickly, this time absent her red wig.

I feel a great weight lifted from my shoulders. Ms Splinters is virtually bald, a condition with which I am sympathetic.

She scratches her scalp. "So you're looking for work at King Korndog, are you?"

"I would like to visit a successful American business, examine the processes, witness it from start to finished product."

"Good idear. Always wise to know what you're getting into. Card never got heard from again, y'know."

"Card is Bena's boy, Mr. Burberry. Graveyard shift chopper hopper operator temp. Missing these many months now."

"Yep. Missing. Started at the slicer dicer, y'know. Well, that wat'n enough of a challenge for him. Always sod after a challenge y'know. That was Card all right. Had the commando spirit, they said. Just had to shift to chopper hopper operator. Well, he drank, y'know."

"Mr. Burberry don't drink, do you, Mr. Burberry?"

"Only when necessary." I show my teeth. The ladies whinny.

"This is a handsome man, Billa. Where'd you find him?"

"He found me, Bena. We're living together, y'know." The ladies nicker louder this time. "Notice his beaver-brown eyes? Word is he might be a prince or a duke." Both ladies examine me from head to toe.

I compliment myself that I had forgotten this morning to install the sea-green or sky-blue lenses as I had intended.

"What is that smell, Bena? I think something's burning!"

"Oh, god! It's my rubbers. I put 'em in the oven to dry 'em off."

"Yep, that's what it smells like. Rubbers, all right."

"Rubbers?" I am at a loss at the expression.

"Uh, you know, rubbers. *Rubbers.*" Mother Crinkle shouts the word, a tactic well used in addressing foreigners in any culture. She then points at her feet, shod now in galoshes.

"Ah. Galoshes. Yes, I understand. Rubbers. My word. Well, live and learn."

"Hey, that's a Balona expression, *live and learn.* I guess you're settling right in here, Mr. Burberry."

"Mother Crinkle, you can call me Silas, mm, Simon, dear."

"Simon. Yeh, well, since we're living together, Simon." Mother Crinkle bats her eyelashes and squeezes my forearm.

Ms Splinters returned wearing unfastened galoshes and an electric-blue print babushka to match the green plastic raincoat draped over her purple muumuu. "I give Sammy Joe Sly a call. Told him I was bringing a distinguished foreign guest for a visit to his plant over there. He said he'd heard all about Mr. Burberry and his trunkful of cash and to bring you on over since he was getting ready to walk the floor himself.

In my Aston-Martin the trip took but two minutes. I was thinking about Madog and about how I must post another card soon to Mum. On the way I noticed people on the sidewalk occasionally shouting and waving their arms. I waved back and put on a happy face. Mother Crinkle mentioned to Ms Splinters, "It'n it cute how he drives on the left-hand side? And what a nice smile!" The two women chortled at my eccentricity and admired my dark English good looks.

We parked in a stall marked Executives, as directed by a little fellow in yellow oilcloth, prominent teeth, and gumboots, he standing on the sidewalk and gesticulating. The chap on the sidewalk turned out to be Mr. Sly himself, owner and operator of King Korndog Inkorporated. He greeted us effusively.

"I been thinking about finding a foreigner, Mr. Burberry." I could not see all of his face clearly because of the rain hood. "I been looking for some good foreign contacts, y'know. Just like you folks look for foreign contacts, y'know. Maybe I got a deal for you! Also, maybe you'd like to join up at Solidarity, a place where you get good *contacts* so you can spend all that cash more wiser, y'know. Well, let's get on in out of the rain."

# 12

## Joseph Oliver Kuhl

Zack has got it into his head that Mr. Burberry is a waiter. The more I think about it—about Mr. Burberry's imagination cover story, the English guy looking for him, the fact that Mr. Burberry is seeking for peace and quiet, his hobby of doing woodworking to take the strain off of his mind, him taking trembling capsules—all that leads me to an inescapable conclusion which I share with Zack.

"Maybe Mr. Burberry's not a real secret agent, but he's not a waiter in disguise, either. If he's not a secret agent, he's actually a writer excaping a nervous breakdown by coming to Balona to build his boxes. I know this from my personal experience writing poems and watching people read 'em." I almost smack my lips since Zack's eyes get big and then squint again. He pooches his lips.

"Well, what do you do to excape your nervous breakdown?"

"Well, I practice zenitation, like Cousin Nim." Actually, it's only Cousin Nim who practices zenitation, but Zack will never know I am putting him on.

"What do you think, Harley? Waiter or writer?"

Harley looks out the window and slowly scratches behind his ear with his hind foot, just like he was ponderating a problem. But of course he does not speak. He does make sort of a groaning noise as he settles down on the window seat.

I explain my rationalization to Zack, watching him carefully for signs of doubt, which he emits frequently about everything.

Zack goes, "Well, Harley says Mr. Burberrry could be a waiter *and* a writer."

"'Harley says.' Stop kidding around, Zack. This is important possible crime busting."

"Who's kidding around. Harley's got one of the best brains in Balona." Harley, closes his eyes, nods into his forepaws. It looks just like he's agreeing with Zack. I could use one of Mr. Burberry's capsules.

Zack continues: "What I been thinking about is Mr. Burberry's interest in chopped-off heads. Maybe he's a serial killer come to this country to excape his just rewards. Maybe he's a waiter-serial killer who is planning to write about his crimes. That's the reason for the notebook where he writes everything down."

"How come Interpol dut'n know about him then, if he's a serial killer?"

"Well, I don't know Interpol dut'n know about him. You don't either. Maybe they do. Maybe they're watching him secretly. Giving him rope to hang himself with, sort of. Or maybe they just don't know he's a serial killer *yet*. Maybe they're waiting for him to do his thing over here, and then they'll nab him."

"The other Englishman, Mr. Madog, had a clipping which showed Mr. Burberry's picture in the paper, but that's all it did: showed his picture. Actually, it just showed a guy looked sort of like Mr. Burberry and called him Silas Blade, but it dit'n say what he was doing in the paper, did it?"

"It's a mystery wrapped in a puzzle."

I knew the famous quotation and completed it for the high school student: "*It's an enigma wrapped in a mystery wrapped in a puzzle wrapped in a condom,* Zack. But I also got some intelligence from Sammy Jack this morning."

"Hey, good work! Anybody who can get intelligence out of Sammy Jack is doing good work. His teachers been trying for years." Zack doesn't think too much of Sam Jack Sly, who is the same age as Zack but is already a second-year student at C4, since he went to a hoity-toity private school where he got promoted and graduated early, since his dad donated generously to the school (according to Sammy Jack himself).

Sam Jack's dad is Sam Joe Sly who is one of the richest guys in Chaud County, Mr. Sly owning the whole King Korndog Korporation and the Kastle Keep down on Eighth Avenue. Mr. Sam Joe Sly gives his kid cars and airplanes and boats and video games and lots of spending money and sends him off by himself to Mexico and France with a pocketful of cash for his vacations.

"So, what about the intelligence you discovered in Sammy Jack?"

"Sam Jack says his dad has invited Mr. Burberry to become a member in Solidarity."

"Everybody knows that, Young Joe. Da mentioned that at breakfast. Usually Da dut'n even know what he's eating any more, but this morning he said about Mr. Burberry and that Mr. Burberry was going to make a fine member since he was so rich." Like a tiny babe, Zack calls his dad *Da* and his ma *Mummy*.

"Sam Jack says that his dad was all impressed at how suave Mr. Burberry is. He said that Mr. Burberry probably will become a binnis advisor to King Korndog Inkorporated, since Mr. Burberry gave Sam Jack's dad some advice about how to save money."

"What advice was that?"

"Sam Jack dit'n say, but he did say that Mr. Burberry wants to learn all the parts of the korndog binnis, starting with the slaughtering part."

"Ugh. I don't ever want to see that part again. Did you ever take the tour over there? The fourth-grade trip to the Kastle Keep?"

Zack didn't have to remind me. I became a vegetablarian practically overnight, since they took us kids through the place where the poor miserable old worn-out dairy cows were being strung up by the back feet, et cetera. They took us all the way through the plant, using a bullhorn to clue us in about what was happening to those skinless corpses. We ended up that part on the catwalk over the barrels of stuff they were saving for a "special run," and we could see eyeballs and stuff floating around in there. A great smell, too. A lot of the kids heaved up their breakfast over the side of the catwalk. Some of the breakfasts ended up in the "special run" barrels.

Then we saw the dogs that become the actual korndogs being squoze and pooped out of a huge machine.

Then we went through the bakery where other big machines were rolling the dogs in dough and putting the raw stuff on monster trays for the baking later. Except they didn't start baking until later, so when we were filing out, a guy stood there and handed each of us a cold day-old korndog to eat *without* Balona Special Sauce on the walk back to school.

On the way back you could see all those cold korndogs in the Eighth Avenue gutter where the kids threw them. When we got back it was lunchtime and guess what we got served for lunch?

Anyway, I have discovered you forget stuff like that when you get hungry. Put enough Balona Special Sauce on a hot korndog, you don't think about the old dead cow hanging there upside down, and you forget about the drums under the catwalk and the "special runs." Amazing what people don't think about.

While Zack was leafing through the copies of Mr. Burberry's notebook, me and him shot the breeze for a while about our korndog-field-trip rememberings, and then I happened to remember. "another thing Sam Jack mentioned this morning. Mr. Burberry was most interested in the chopper hopper."

"Hm? Mr. Burberry maybe wants to be chopper hopper operator? That's pretty technical work, and dangerous, I heard."

"Well, Sammy Jack said that Mr. Burberry's going to be like a temp. Spend time learning about all the machines and the ovens over there. So he can be a top-level advisor to Mr. Sly. That's what Sammy Jack says his dad said."

"I wonder how Mr. Burberry got into Mr. Sly's confidence so soon."

"Probably it's his UITS training. I have noticed some other tradecraft-type manifestations."

"He still stands like a waiter."

"I believe he is collecting information for an important book he's writing. Maybe on American binnis." A thought occurs and I could feel my whole body cool off. "I wonder if it is possible...."

"What? What? You're looking like you just saw a ghost."

"I wonder if he could be an *industrial* spy! Sucking secrets out of King Korndog to take back to his foreign land and so on."

"What about the boxes?"

"Oh, the boxes. Well, maybe he'll put korndog samples in those boxes. Or formulas. Or the Balona Secret Sauce recipe. Or secret photographs of how they do it all." It all fits. All of it came to me in a rush. "All that cash in his briefcase is for bribing King Korndog workers to reveal their secrets. Any Balona guy would be happy to get bribed."

"Well, it's possible he's not a waiter after all. But he still stands that way, as you may well know." This is Zack's way of saying that maybe I have made a point. Suddenly Zack exclaims and Harley looks up, interested. "Hey! Listen to this. Another one of Mr. Burberry's things copied from somewhere:

> *Gunther von Hagens believes that his system of plastination—preserving the flesh of actual corpses by removing the water and injecting polymers—helps people appreciate the natural*

*beauty of their bodies. That means seeing just what the body looks like, minus skin and fat, and helping to ease some of the natural fear of death and decay."*

Zack gives me his *weird* look, the one he's been perfecting for years, designed to scare little kids into giving him their lunch money. Of course, since he is reformed, he no longer uses it on little kids, he says, except the occasional freshman. "So what about this, I wonder!" Zack shuffles through more pages. "Here's a copy of a letter Mr. Burberry wrote to Mr. von Hagens asking him for the formula. Wow. The letter is signed *Silas Blade*."

"Well, that's Mr. Burberry's cover name, of course. But plasterfication it'n a subject a waiter would be interested in. A writer might be interested, though. Right?"

"Or a serial killer, as you may well know."

"It could tie in with industrial espionage, though. Like, Mr. Burberry could be planning to worm out the secrets of the korndog, spirit them away to England, make himself a fortune."

"How do you figure plastinating a korndog will make him a fortune?"

"Well, I don't know. How should I know? We're just trying to figure stuff out here, not solving a crime."

"Not solving a crime—yet!"

Zack always makes everything into a big drama. But actually I am worried now. This case is developing into something manifestly sinister. But I shall put all my training to work and solve this puzzle. First, though, I better see that I don't get kicked out of C4 since I have missed a few classes lately.

# 13

## Simon Burberry

I feel almost Californian, not to say American this day, for I have been inducted as a brother into Solidarity. Mr. Sam Joe Sly, my sponsor, transported me to Delta City in his Rolls, a very special surprise. He drove the car himself, mentioning that his chauffeur had "the flu" and was indisposed this morning.

"I'm rich enough to afford a cook and a maid, too, but I don't bother, since I'm on the road a lot, and them people would just steal you blind." Mr. Sly is no longer married, and his one son is often "out on his own." Thus, the Sly mansion is largely unattended. "C'mon over to the mansion any time. I don't gotta be there. The key's under the mat. Make yourself t'home."

Friendly chap. His opinion of people in service seems to be generally bleak, for he spoke also of butlers and gardeners and housekeepers as generally unreliable. I have not found the case to be true, but then, he was speaking of American domestics, a group with whom I am not at all familiar. Then, too, I must admit, Britain has seen some change in domestic temperament.

Mr. Sly is a short fellow with an adenoidal catarrh problem, relieved periodically by great snorting and clearing of passages. He has a distinctly weasel-like appearance, even as to posture. He excused himself for conferring on his cell phone during much of our trip to Delta City, and on the return trip as well. He dictated orders, remonstrated with inferiors, spoke of money matters, and generally behaved like the CEO he is. But of course I gave no indication that I heard a word. In fact, the trips gave opportunity for me to review in my mind's eye my enlightening and stimulating visit to the King Korndog Kastle Keep.

When Mr. Sly ushered us into his office that day, I felt for a moment that I had re-entered the Royal Pavilion at Brighton: every sort of gew-gaw imaginable was displayed on tables, racks, shelves, in frames, bottles, vases, et cetera. The stuffed heads of animals, wild and domestic, were peering from the walls, high and low. These caught my attention at once, of course, and I inquired about the technique of taxidermy generally employed in this area.

"Hell, I dunno. I just shoot 'em and eat 'em. I don't stuff 'em. Binky Swainhammer is the stuffer." He then laughed uproariously, inciting Mmes. Crinkle and Splinters to displays of mirth. We all laughed. I did not ask about the stuffed head of what was clearly a dairy cow, possibly a Guernsey, mounted over the door to the office, but he caught my attentive glance and explained.

"She's a looker, eh? Got her head off of the floor out there. Too dang nice to chop up." This poor beast evidently was a superannuated milk producer, the rest of whose corpse became part of the King Korndog product. "We send our korndogs all over the world nowdays, y'know. Except to your country. You heard what I'm saying? *Except to your country?* And we grind in pork and mutton, too, y'know, whenever we need to fill a quota. King Korndog's not prejudice. It's just that we don't label our stuff anything but beef, so the ragheads don't get upset. We don't bleed enough for real Jews, so only jack-Jews eat korndog anyhow." He snorted again and laughed loudly. Mmes. Crinkle and Splinters joined him. I smiled reservedly, considering bleeding processes in general.

Mr. Sly handed me what he called a slicker and a pair of gumboots. "We gonna get juicy out there, so you better put these on. You ladies, you just stay right here and drink coffee from the pot over there. But don't eat up all the danish! Me and Mr. Burberry here's gonna take us a little tour."

At our first of many stops, a grain truck was unloading bulk corn. "This is a for-profit company, Mr. Burberry, so we do use a little filler along with the meat. Say, you don't mind I call you Simon, do you?"

I allowed as how that could be allowed.

I won't go on very precisely about the rest of the facility. Suffice it to say it is not different from Mr. Prothero's small facility, except as to King Korndog's scale and the complexity of the tools employed. The extent of that part of the operation was nothing but spectacular. Mr. Prothero's stuffing operation is piddling in contrast, if effective. The capsule I had taken before breakfast did not diminish the effect.

The chopper hopper Mother Crinkle and Ms Splinters had alluded to was a huge fearsome machine, replete with knobs, buttons, wheels, levers, and dials on a control board, attended by a fellow perched on what appeared to be a rather insubstantial tractor seat suspended quiveringly over a great vat. Pipes gurgled overhead, discharging hot water and other fluids from monstrous bins at the attendant's command. The chopper hopper whirred. Giant blades swirled and gnashed the contents of the vat.

"Okay, so you can still see a few bones down in there. But this is where, I guarantee you, everything gets ground up nice and fine. We don't waste nothing." Mr. Sly rubbed his thumb and forefinger together to symbolize the making of money.

The chopper hopper operator did not deign to wear his safety belt, but smoked his cigar undaunted by the confusion around him. The steam generated was roseate and redolent of the spices which were undoubtedly being added to the blood-rich blend.

I thought to myself, *Here is a position which allows and demands that one be in complete control in order to produce a product to be admired by one and all.* No room for error. No room for lack of concentration. I thought, This is one job Burberry might perform without cavil. Blade would be jealous.

Mr. Sly was watching me. "Impressive, huh! I cut'n stand it up there, though. Like being on a rope dangling from Yosemite, y'know. And lonesome at night if we're rushed and you gotta work then. Also, I wanna be where you make money, not mush!" I could not hear his laughter, but I could see its many manifestations. We then went on finally to visit the bakery, with its dough-making machinery, all automated, and the great ovens, automated but not yet fired. It was all impressive.

The chopper hopper operation had been most impressive.

"My, you smell like korndog," remarked Mother Crinkle when we had settled again in my car. I was not sure if that were to be taken as a compliment.

"Is that a good smell?" I asked, employing the vernacular.

"Oh, my, yes! That's a true Balona smell!"

We had korndogs for lunch that day, as usual. I disciplined myself not to think of the Guernsey over the door.

The Solidarity breakfast for which my sponsor paid the fee offered korndogs as well. But I was pleased to see Solidaritans lined up for the traditional English breakfast. Actually, I should say a *Scots* breakfast, for it included oatmeal in addition to kippers and bangers, rashers of bacon in the hundreds, eggs in all styles, and toast, as well as stewed figs (which I found something of a novelty); and prunes (which, after frequent meals of korndogs and cabbage, I do not require).

After prayers and flag salutes, mumbled announcements, and reports from a variety of sources, I was introduced, receiving considerable applause which surprised me. Asked to "say a few words," I recited some lines from Kipling (about friendship, hands across the seas, the honor of being honored, service, honor again, and solidarity in general). I sat down to tumultuous applause followed at once by a standing ovation and a spontaneous rendering of *God Save the Queen* (with words I did not recognize).

Among those present were Sheriff Chaud, who did not at first recognize me until I flashed my Anson Chaud for Sheriff button which I had fastened to the underside of my lapel, the side opposite my badge. Kenworth Kuhl closed his eyes and frowned when he saw me, then brightened as if recognizing an old friend. A wizened fellow who was introduced to me as Mr. D. H. Carp is a Balona grocer, member of the Balona Town Council, and a perennial candidate for the American Congress.

The meeting was over within an hour and included a speech by a Mr. Kenworth Burnross. The Burnross name is familiar. Mr. Burnross lost his rhetorical way immediately after the introductory part of his address, looked fixedly at the ceiling, asked if this was "the Veterans" meeting, and sat again to his korndogs.

After the meeting I made my way to Mr. Burnross still at his breakfast. I introduced myself and mentioned that one could always use the services of a good solicitor and, given that I was considering the possibility of settling down in Balona., I asked would he be professionally free. Mr. Burnross smiled vacantly, found a business card for me in his vest. I made an appointment with him for this afternoon that I hope he might remember.

Mr. Sly soon had my elbow in his grasp and was steering me toward the exit. Mr. Carp approached and rasped, "You interested in politics, are you? Somebody said you was interested in politics. That's what I heard."

"I have never held public office."

"Well, you wanna think about it, a guy with your style. You oughta run for office." He squeezed my bicep several times.

"I'm an Englishman, sir, not a citizen of the United States, not a long-time resident of Balona."

"Hell, that don't make no difference in Balona, providing you got style—and are flexible. I notice you dit'n say you *wat'n* interested." He raised his eyebrows and winked a pale gray eye. Flexibility may be the condition to consider here. Perhaps Balona politics are no different from county politics at home, where flexibility is requisite and well known.

"I am in Balona on a kind of rest tour, sir. I should wish to be as inconspicuous as possible."

"Yeh, I heard ya. You could rest right on the job in Balona, long as you was flexible. Just think about the possibilities." Mr. Carp walked off to shake hands with everyone in sight.

Mr. Sly looked at me from the corner of his eye. "When Mr. D. H. Carp takes an interest in a guy, the guy is maybe got some political potential, y'know. Now Mr. D. H. Carp himself, he's got no political potential at all, but he's got a good eye. You really oughta think about them possibilities. Y'know we got a mayor to elect pretty soon."

Mayor Burberry of Balona. In the Sly-driven car on the way back to Balona, I grew all warm and furry inside, just thinking about myself in a mayor's gown, key on a gold chain about my neck, being flexible, resting. Madog and Blight would be green with envy. Thought of Madog and concern that he might be continuing his search caused an abrupt surge of peptic gas, and I had to excuse my rude exhalation.

"Don't think nothing of it. Korndogs'll do it ever time. Just goes to show you're getting to be a regular Balona guy." My host-driver went on to bolster his recommendation that I consider running for office in Balona. "You got style, Mr. Burberry, uh Simon. I mean you even belch with style, and that'll get you votes so you don't have to make no promises at all. Just stand there and press the flesh. No advertising necessary. No campaign. Just word of mouth. No filing fee in Balona. You just go over to Mr. D. H. Carp's place there on Front Street and tell him you wanna sign up. That's it. Easy as pie." He smacked the steering wheel with evident delight. "And you get to take a nice salary, too. For doing nothing at all. Well, not exactly nothing at all. You do got to be flexible."

Flexibility again.

I could envision myself striding the Front Street sidewalks in my blond wig with the sky-blue lenses, "pressing the flesh," kissing babies, et cetera, collecting a nice salary, doing nothing at all, except being flexible and making more boxes as they might become necessary. Perhaps I shall take my capsules regularly and retire from box-making.

No, not the blond wig. I would need to confirm a persona that is already well established. I would need to wear the black-and-brown for the rest of my stay. I could do worse with my time. The prospect of appropriate office has become definitely interesting.

A police car was parked in front of the Crinkle residence when Mr. Sly deposited me. A riding lawn mower machine was parked in the driveway, not quite touching the bumper of my own vehicle. A very large blue-uniformed man sat on the seat of the police car, its door open. The large fellow was eating something from a paper sack. He folded the top of the sack and greeted me as Mr. Sly drove slowly away, Mr. Sly's head twisted behind him so as to see what was happening at his rear.

"You Mr. Burberry?"

"Yes, Officer. Yes, I am he."

"That your mower there?"

"No, sir. I have not seen that machine before." The machine was obviously new, its paint bright green, yellow and white tags fluttering from its handles.

"It's stole from back of Mr. D. H. Carp's Groceries and Sundries." The officer set his bag aside and threw himself violently out of the vehicle toward the gutter, thus enabling him to rise to an erect posture. He gasped and wheezed piteously.

"Ah, well. I notice that the thief left it where it could be reclaimed with ease."

"Yeh. Guess so. You dit'n steal it? Feller at my office said he seen you steal it from behind Mr. D. H. Carp's place, y'know."

"Impossible, sir. I have been with Mr. Sam Joe Sly at a Solidarity meeting in Delta City all morning. Mr. Sly has just this moment returned me to this spot, as you have seen."

"Well, then, cut'n be you, I guess." He looked at the mower. "I guess you wut'n be interested in riding it back up to Mr. D. H. Carp's then."

"I am not familiar with the mechanism, sir."

"Not familiar. Well, I guess I'll go brace Mr. Blight and fy to trigger out what's the score here."

Ah! First Madog. Now Blight has discovered me. Can others be far behind?

# 14

### Joseph Oliver Kuhl

What has happened is almost un-thinkable not to say unbelievable, so I'm having to drink another Hires to think about it and maybe really get to believe it. I came to hear about it sort of second-hand, from my usual spot on the landing during one of my ma's bridge mornings.

Since it's semester break for us C4 scholars, it wasn't necessary for me to attend classes, so I slept in and then took a nice long hot shower. A safe shower since Richie wasn't home to run around and turn on all the hot-water taps in the house so as to turn me into an ice cube from the shower water.

Richie is a rude person and regularly does that sort of thing, especially on poor old Dad. Or he will sneak in the bathroom, take the paper off of the roll, dunk it in the toilet till it's soaked through, and put it back on the roller. Or, while you're in the shower stall he will take away all the towels and your clothes. Then when you grope your way out of the shower, you have to prance down the hall dripping in your birthday suit to the linen closet to find something to dry off with.

I made a New Year's resolution to figure out a way to take Richie down a peg or two. Only I haven't figured out a way to do that yet. I'm working at it. First, I got to figure out a way to take Zack down a peg or two, and then Patella.

Back to the un-thinkable.

I was sitting on the landing out of sight, drinking a Hires and eating a horse derve. Also skimming over my UITS Manual. This book is full of useful tradecraft, and it pays for an agent to skim over it every once in a while. I can understand why Mr. Burberry had it on top of all the stuff in his briefcase. For example, it tells you to Listen with Care and Remember. I don't always remember everything, so I do what else it says: Take Careful Notes.

Actually, at first there wasn't a whole lot to Listen with Care about at the bridge tables, and so I didn't Take Careful Notes, either. Instead, like I said, I was skimming the Manual. The bridge players sounded a lot like clones of Bootsie Dwindle's ma, sort of like chickens. All were talking at once, the way women do when supposedly listening to each other and at the same time trying to get their own word in edgewise. Balona guys, on the other hand, do the opposite. They give the impression they're actually listening to the other guys (really they're figuring out what they are going to say next), and then they horn in at the first gasp in the conversation.

With a group of Balona women talking together, you have the impression of a constant squawking, like musical instruments tuning up. I use this musical comparison since I have been trying to figure out how *The Rite of Spring* is so noisy in its great way. With Balona guys in a group, you hear one guy's solid sentence, followed by another guy's one, with practically no breathing in between. Not musical at all. Maybe just percussion.

The squawking was considerably louder at this game, since it was two tables and the women happened to be the louder women of Balona. My ma can be louder than anybody, so I won't even count her. But she was one. Another one was Aunt Pippa, who is actually Great-Aunt Pippa, even though she's younger than my ma. But I won't go on to explain that, except to say that Aunt Pippa's dad was my famous Great-Grandpa Julius Caesar Kuhl who produced kids well into his 90s—a real vigorous guy. Aunt Pippa has a high voice so, while it isn't real loud, is kind of like a siren sound, going up and down in a whiney way.

Aunt Sarah (who is only a Kuhl cousin, not an aunt at all) is Cod's ma. She sounds more more like a man. She even has a sort of mustache that may contribute to her bassoon sound. Bellona Shaw talks through her nose, like an oboe, so you can hear her above most, except not over my ma. That's just one table.

The second table included Anna Trilbend and Mrs. Eg Sasifrage, both rich. Mrs. Trilbend is Mr. Frag Trilbend's new wife, and he just built her a huge new house up on the West Levee Road, him being the manager of the Balona Branch of the Bank of the Delta. She sounds like a piccolo or a guinea pig in pain.

Mrs. Sasifrage's husband is the new president of the Merchants and Ranchers Bank, since the old president got sent to jail for embezzlement and fraud, et cetera. Mrs. Sasifrage, "Phoebe," moved here from Delta City and sounds like a trumpet. Not as loud as Ma, but you can hear her, no problem.

I tell all this stuff about husbands and musical instruments because a lot of the conversations at these games always has to do with one woman getting over on another one, usually about a husband.

For example, my ma started off by pointing out that Mrs. Anna Trilbend is always referring to herself as Mrs. *Anna* Trilbend rather than as Mrs. Fragonard Trilbend. "How come you don't give old Frag his due, Anna?"

"He says I shut'n hide my light under a bushel is why, if it's any of your binnis. He's a New Man. He dut'n believe in keeping a woman barefoot and pregnant." My ma happens to be habitually barefoot, if not pregnant. It isn't usually wise to talk back this way to my ma, but Mrs. Trilbend isn't all that experienced, which I guess is why my ma refrained from grabbing her by her hair and throwing her down the front steps.

Mrs. Bellona Shaw (there doesn't seem to be a Mr. Shaw) always talks about Mr. Don Keyshot, a counselor at Big Baloney who got fired and now helps guys with problems. "Don is a New Man, too, y'know. He's always going on so about how I should put myself forth more."

My ma went, "That hair-do puts yourself forth, I'd say." All the voices at both tables agreed for once.

"Well, he gives good advice. You women ought to consider going to him for advice when you have problems." Mrs. Shaw is touting Mr. Keyshot's counseling services. "He dut'n charge any more than those quacks in Delta City, either."

"I just ast Cleo here when I got problems, and Cleo pours me a libration and tells me to forget it." My ma was referring to Mrs. Earwick who was pouring coffee. It just happens that Mrs. Earwick is Mrs. Anna Trilbend's grandmother, but neither one of them will even look at the other. My ma says it's because Mrs. Trilbend "married up" and her grandma is too far beneath her to recognize.

Mrs. Earwick is also about a 100 years old, wears bright red lipstick, lacy dresses and spike heels, and is always about to fall down from the bottle she nips on in the kitchen. Mrs. Earwick didn't say anything. Just cackled, an appropriate sound.

Mrs. Shaw went on about Mr. Keyshot. "I advised Don he should run for mayor, since he's got a lot of class and everybody knows he's honest, eksedra. He'd win hands down."

"He talks too much and he's not flexible enough. Everybody knows that. In Balona, the mayor's got to be flexible." Aunt

Sarah smacked her lips, kind of like Zack or his dad does. This smack was probably a horse-derve smack.

Mrs. Shaw dropped her bomb. "Well, Don would make a great mayor if he was a bit more flexible. But the truth is, it's Mr. Burberry who's going to be our next mayor."

There was a collection of gasps and snorts.

"Well, he's certainly got style," Mrs. Trilbend admitted. "I'd probably vote for him."

The two other women at Anna Trilbend's and Phoebe Sasifrage's table are skinny Mrs. Billa Crinkle and fat Mrs. Bena Splinters, both of them wearing muumuus and both of them really old. I mean *old*. So old that Ma is referring to the table as the Senior Table, even though Mrs. Trilbend and Mrs. Sasifrage are younger than Ma.

Mrs. Crinkle spoke right up about Mr. Burberry. "He's not only got style, he's got me!" She cackled like she was about to lay an egg. She was joined in the cackling by Mrs. Splinters who is famous in Balona for being as big as my ma, but nowhere near as strong, of course.

My ma pursued the interrogation. "Well, Bellona, where'd you hear that about Mr. Burberry?"

"I heard it direct from Mr. D. H. Carp, about five minutes before I got here, so it's fresh news you ladies are hearing. When we quit here, I'm going back to the office and write up my column which will blow the lid off of this election."

"What's there to blow off?"

"Well, the fact that somebody besides members of the Town Council is running for mayor."

"Whoever is mayor is a member of the council."

"Well, I know that."

"Well, you make it sound like a big revolution. Alls Mr. Burberry has to do to run is sign up at Mr. D. H. Carp's. Anybody can do that. That don't mean he's gonna be the next mayor."

"Mr. Burberry has style. Around here, what with the likely competition, he'll win hands down."

"Not elbows down, though!" My ma was referring to her easy victory over Mr. Burberry at the arm-wrestling competition in this very house.

"Show us the tape again, Bapsie!"

So the ladies took a break and watched my ma banquish Mr. Burberry is less than a minute, him looking like Rocky Balboa after the tenth round.

Mrs. Sasifrage went, "I wonder."

Nobody paid much attention, except women can never stand not knowing what another woman was going to say. So all you have to do with a woman is say, "I wonder…." and then look sort of puzzled. She will right away force you to reveal what you were wondering about. This is something I learned very early on in my life so far.

So, even though nobody was paying attention, the remark was noted subcutaneously, and pretty soon Mrs. Bellona Shaw leaned across to the other table and like, "Well, what is it you were wondering, Phoebe? Tell us, for heavensakes!"

"Well, I was just wondering if Mr. Burberry will have any competition. I mean, Pippa's husband wut'n run, since he's so old and decrepit."

Then there was five minutes of argument about Uncle Kenworth Burnross's mental condition. There were some contributions by Mrs. Crinkle and Mrs. Splinters about the weirdnesses exhibited by their own late husbands. Then five more minutes of Aunt Pippa sobbing and being comforted about her ancient husband's probable loss of mind. All this time Mrs. Shaw was writing like mad in her notebook. Mrs. Earwick came in with more horse-derves and coffee, this time also with a bottle of brandy which she comforted Aunt Pippa with a shot from in her coffee cup. After which Mrs. Anna Trilbend piped up with the shocker.

"I know who could take Mr. Burberry, hands down."

All the ladies stopped talking. That is always a shocker in itself, but it wasn't the shocker I am referring to.

"Who?" everybody went, like a choir of owls slightly out of synch.

"Her." Mrs. Anna Trilbend was pointing at my ma.

"Bapsie?"

Nobody spoke a word for about 10 seconds. Then they all laughed. Mrs. Shaw spoke first. "I almost thought you serious there for a moment, Anna."

"Oh, but I was. Bapsie is perfect for mayor. Nobody would ever accuse her of not being flexible or they'd get a poke on the nose." Everybody laughed. "She would make those old farts on the council shape up where Mr. Burberry would just be a fashion-place, noble-looking and polite." Nobody laughed, just looked at my ma.

My ma was looking into her coffee cup, smirking to herself. "I could make up some new rules and regulations, too, huh!"

"You wut'n actually run for office, would you Bapsie?" This from Mrs. Shaw.

"Why not!" went Mrs. Sasifrage.

"Why not!" went Mrs. Crinkle, "except you cut'n let on that I betrayed my Mr. Burberry."

"Why not!" went Mrs. Splinters. "Who're we talking about here anyways?" Mrs. Splinters was sounding a little like Uncle Kenworth Burnross.

"Well, Bapsie?"

"I never give it a thought, but why not? Yeh. Why not!"

That was the shocker: My ma is going to run for mayor. Against Mr. Burberry. Since I am now a registered voter myself, with Kuhl Blood (sang froyd) running in my veins as well as my ma's Chaud Blood, I will soon have to make a decision.

# 15

### Simon Burberry

"It's quite nice to be spoken to politely, for a change." This with a smile from the Front Street chemist known to Balonans as *Hank.* I refer to him as *Mr. Vibrissa* rather than *Hank.* He is pleased. He is not native to Balona.

"Mr. Vibrissa, I have a list of items perhaps you can supply me with in small amounts. I don't need them by the litre!" We both chuckle.

He squints at my list. "Oh? Yeh, I've got some of this stuff handy right here, and I can get you the rest in a couple days." He has a quizzical expression now. "You an engineer of some kind, Mr. Burberry?"

"Oh, I merely dabble and experiment, y'know."

"Ah. Sure."

"And, Mr. Vibrissa, I also have a capsule here, but no prescription to go with it as the documentation was lost during my journey. I'm wondering if you are able to determine its composition and dosage, et cetera, and provide me with a supply for a month or so.

"Well, now, I can look at it and see it in the catalog easy enough, if it's there, Mr. Burberry, but I cut'n give you a supply without the prescription." I allow my facial expression to compose itself into one of tragic concern. "But I could maybe give you a few advance capsules, y'know, until your new prescription comes through. Tide you over, y'know." He holds the capsule up to the light. "Yeh, I think I could do that." He frowns. "Say, I gotta tell you I'm not familiar with this capsule, but I will look it up if you'll give me a few minutes."

"Ah, it may not be listed in the pharmacopeia, Mr. Vibrissa, for it may include herbal substances."

"Herbal? I don't do herbal stuff, Mr. Burberry." He winks. "Except a little Mary Jane for relaxation purposes, y'know."

"Perhaps you could break open a capsule and from the odor and appearance discern the composition?"

"Uh, well, I could try. Probably your best bet for herbal stuff would be the Chinese place in Delta City. Well, I'll open it here and take a look. Jeez, this does have quite a smell. I don't recognize it though."

I observe aloud that the weather looks as if the sun might shine soon, but Mr. Vibrissa returns my capsule, shakes his head dolefully, and remarks that the sun never shines in February in Balona so that one can see it.

I replace the capsule in my capsule box, rubbing the familiar round little box in my fingers and considering my plight. Actually various plights. Doctor Schimpf has remarked that I am *compulsive*. That is very true, but that condition is in itself not very serious. That is, it does not obstruct or impede any important activity.

So I must put on my trousers only after I put on my shoes, and always the left trouser leg first. I must draw on my left sock first, but my right shoe on first. I must always lick the envelope flap before I insert the letter. I must sleep on the door-nearer side of any bed. I must sit in any restaurant booth with my back to a wall, but being seated at a counter causes little distress. Of course I must wear my Argylles to bed, whatever the weather. Occasionally upon awakening I will find gravel in my socks, testimony to the sleepwalking I am prone to.

Another plight I must now consider is the postcards I have been sending to Mum since my flight. It has occurred to me that anyone who wished to discover my present location had only to filch those cards from Mum's postbox and examine the postmark to arrive at the answer. Perhaps that is what Madog did, and then passed on the information to the execrable Blight.

Blight still reposes chained in the back room of the constable's office. In idle recent conversation with Joseph Kuhl I learned that this is not an unusual circumstance. Balona lawbreakers before time have been subjected to the same fate if they contest the constable's judgment. The lawman simply waits them out, and as the miserable criminals grow thin and pale, their wrists chafed and their bowels bound by the bread, cheese, and water diet he inflicts upon them, they eventually agree to the imposed fine, pay the sum, and are released.

Blight, of course, is stubborn. He probably believes that in the New World this imprisonment is illegal and that he will be rescued soon. Joseph tells me that Constable Cod is still formulating the theft charges, and that writing them out is a task that will take the constable more time yet.

After the charges are brought, Cod will transport Blight to the County Jail, a facility presided over by Sheriff Anson Chaud, said to be a blood relation to the Balona constable. I have not laid eyes upon Blight, and don't intend to. The longer he is detained, the better. Whenever the constable sees me on the street, he tips his cap. Word of my candidacy has spread.

"Yeh, alls you gotta do is sign here, Mr. Burberry." Thus spake Mr. D. H. Carp, allowing me to use his pen to affix my signature to the application for office.

"Must I not be registered to vote?"

"Nah. You just come on in on election day and put your X where it belongs. That's good enough for us. We're not proud. We don't hold with hoity-toity." Mr. Carp also presented other protestations of his flexibility regarding procedures.

A woman I did not at once recognize approached me in the market, pen and notebook in hand, just as I had completed the application. It was the redheaded woman of the newspaper office, now a blonde-haired person with red lips of remarkable hue. Red lips alone do not precipitate the trembling.

"You have just applied to be part of the election," she announced. She examined my face keenly. "They *are* brown," she muttered.

"Yes, Mrs....?

"Shaw. Bellona Shaw. It's spelled with an ee and two ells. Bellona, I mean, not Shaw. Different than the town name, of course. And Shaw is spelled just the way you might think, the way the English author is spelled."

I did not correct her ethnic misperception, although the compulsion to do so lurked just under my breath.

"Yes, Mrs. Shaw. I have applied." I showed my teeth. "Perhaps I can count on your vote?"

"Well, I'll need to know something of your platform."

I thought rapidly, a characteristic I have been burnishing since my acquisition of the Manual. "I intend to be flexible!"

"Ah, good. That's a characteristic said to be absolutely necessary in any Balona mayor."

"I wonder if I could ask you a question, dear lady." I leaned forward a bit and twinkled at her.

"My! Dear lady, indeed! Of course you may."

89

"Can you tell me what my duties as mayor might be? No one seems to know."

"Well, you preside over Town Council meetings. But I have never been to a Town Council meeting, so I do not know exactly what that might entail. As I have been given to understand, Balona hasn't had a public Town Council meeting for some years."

"Ah. Well, that explains part of my concern."

"What might be the other concern?"

"It's a bit embarrassing to discuss."

"I am discreet as anybody in town."

"It is the emolument."

"The what?"

"How much is the mayor paid?"

"Oh. That's the good part. The mayor himself gets to decide." Mrs. Shaw looked at the ceiling. "Or I should say the mayor himself *or herself*, shut'n I?"

I chuckled. "Oh, indeed. Politically correct, and all."

"Yes, but also accurate. Do you know who your competition will be?"

"Yes, I see." I did not perceive her point, but I let it go in the interest of getting home to my car and search for my missing keys so as to drive to Delta City and explore the Chinese pharmacy there. "Thank you, dear lady, for your kind information."

Mrs. Shaw tittered, put away her pen and notebook. "We need to sit down for a real interview, Mr. Burberry."

"Of course, as long as you do not print it. I'm incognito, you know, as I am being pursued by assassins."

Mrs. Shaw looked at me as if I were daft. She smiled. She frowned. Her eyebrows rose and fell. Her bosom rose and fell. "Are you serious? You're not serious!"

"I am serious. Good day."

"My goodness. My goodness. Law!"

I tipped my hat before leaving. This simple act seems to surprise Balonans, perhaps because of all the male residents here only one, Mr. Kenworth Burnross, wears a hat, and he is said often to forget he is wearing it.

Leaving Mr. D. H. Carp's establishment and preparing to cross Front Street, I tripped and fell to one knee in the gutter, making a tiny gash in my trouser fabric. As I am an excellent seamster, I anticipated no problem in mending the tear. But at home in the Crinkle house, my knee medicated, bandaged, and bare, and seated at last on my bed with needle and thread, I was surprised by a visit from Mother Crinkle.

"You sure got nice knees, Mr. Burberry. A little skinny on top there, but nice knees." She sat on the bed next to me. "You ever think of marriage, Mr. Burberry, uh, Simon?"

I confessed that in my business, marriage was inadvisable.

"What binnis is that, Simon?"

"Well, one might say I'm in the mayor business." I was using a clever tradecraft response, but she found it humourous.

"Yeh, you might be. You might be. Well, you just keep on thinking about maybe getting married to a mature person who could appreciate your peculiarities. And also leave you a nice house and a good bank account when she pushes off, if you know what I mean."

Mother Crinkle appeared to be proposing marriage, not a situation with which I am unfamiliar. I set down my needle and patted her hand. "I shall certainly think about it, Mother Crinkle. Maturity does offer vastly more advantages than barriers, I should think." I picked up my needle and began whistling my tune, despite my determination not to.

"What a nice tune. I heard it before, a long time ago. What is that tune you whistle so nice?"

"I cannot for the life of me remember the title, but it fills my head at certain times and I cannot extirpate it." I continued whistling, but softer, quite expertly. I should try to apply for an American telly show where one displays one's talents. I should win a prize I think.

"You whistle real good, Mr. Burberry. You not only got style, you whistle real good. Maybe you'll be mayor, too. A whistling mayor. Providing you win."

Madog has disappeared. Blight is chained to the wall in the constable's back room. I am almost out of capsules. The whistling helps relieve the potential of trembling. I resolved to drive to Delta City and find the Chinese pharmacy as soon as possible.

# 16

### Joseph Oliver Kuhl

Now that I have been shocked to the depths of my sole, I needed to see what my dad would say about Barbara Balona "Bapsie" Chaud-Kuhl as Mayor of Balona.

"Huh?" is all Dad said at first. Then, "You're kidding, right?"

"No, Dad. She seems to be determined to go into politics."

"Oh, well. I won't be interference for her." Dad sometimes uses terms that have a couple of meanings, so you never really know where he stands on subjects. He just shook out his *Courier* and started to read, frowning and squinting because he can't find his glasses. Mrs. Shaw will probably write up a couple of columns, and Mr. Pat Preene will have his editorial say, too. Even Patella will get her licks in.

That got me thinking that, as long as it was semester break, with no brain-busting studies to dwell into, maybe I could write a column supporting my ma's candidacy. Or not supporting it. If my column supported it, I would get laughed out of town. Or if my column didn't support it, I could get thrown down the front steps by my hair. So, thinking about all the brain strain and labor involved, and the fact that I had to get to my part-time job at Mr. D. H. Carp's, I decided not to write any column at all. Instead, I would just think thoughts about writing a column.

Anyway, the *Courier* didn't yet have anything about candidates in it. Most of the paper was devoted to the story about how a bunch of sheep got stolen from the King Korndog readypens, and how nobody saw 40 sheep being herded down Eighth Avenue in the middle of the night all the way over to a vacant lot on Airport Way. You could see Mr. Pat Preene's photo of big tire tracks in the mud, along with evidence left by a sheep. Mr. Preene had a huge headline across the front page calling the theft, "Daring Balona Mystery! Arabs Suspected!" Just goes to show that when Balona sleeps, we sleep deep.

Sure thing that happened next was Mrs. Shaw squealed her tires in front of the house. She came racing up to the front door and rapped her umbrella handle on it, since she knows the door bell doesn't work. After she knocked, she came right on in, feeling I guess that as a bridge player, she could be at home in Kuhl Mansion. Lucky my ma was in the bathroom and not in the living room when our unexpected visitor showed up and plonked herself breathing hard onto our expensive new leather couch (which we bought when we were rich and isn't paid for).

"Well, Joseph," she gasped, not smiling since she gives the impression she doesn't like me much, for what reason I don't know. Maybe because I didn't give her a big lie about how suave her new hairdo looks. "I need to see Bapsie about a column I'm working on." Mrs. Shaw was wearing a black sweat suit and big white Air Jordans with yellow socks. A real Balona fashion place.

So I went and pounded on the bathroom door, not always a good idea when you know your ma is in there. I hollered at the door that she had a guest with a notebook and a purple pen ready to make her famous. Immediately lots of flushing.

"So, you're gonna make me famous, my chief *dum-shik* here says." My ma uses home-made cuss words, believing that they are more high-class than the regular Balona cuss words guys use around here.

"Well, I thought maybe you'd like to give me some choice tidbits that would give your candidacy a boost." Mrs. Shaw squinched up her mouth and eyebrows in a smile that my ma immediately made an imitation of. Ma is a great imitator of face expressions and voices. She can sound like practically anybody. What is amazing about her imitations is that when she does them, the person she does it about never recognizes the imitation.

"Well, Bellona, first off, I'm gonna beat the *pooper-scoop* out of that wimp."

"Only literally speaking, of course, I hope. I heard you are planning a debate."

"What debate? Who said anything about a debate? You mean where you get up and make speeches? I'm not gonna make any speeches at all. I'm just gonna beat that wimp Burberry. Hands down. His shoes are always shiny. What a wimp! I bet he's got Billa Crinkle down on her beat-up old knees polishing his shoes. Where'd you hear I was gonna debate?" Ma was starting to sound fierce.

"Oh, I don't know. I just heard it. Maybe Anna Trilbend said something."

"Anna don't know her *addlebass* from first base. What's she know about debates? What's she know about Balona politics? Anna Trilbend don't know *diddley-poodley*."

"As I recall, it was Anna Trilbend who first mentioned you as a viable candidate for mayor. Of course, I have also heard her praising Mr. Burberry."

"Who needs her! I'll get voted on by the whole town. Just wait and see. Won't nobody vote for a *dum-shik* foreigner. Everybody knows you gotta be flexible to be mayor in Balona. Everybody knows how flexible I am. Everybody knows foreigners aren't flexible at all." My ma takes a long pull on her glass of hot toddy. Even though the morning is cold and there's plenty to share, she hasn't offered a glass to Mrs. Shaw. Mrs. Shaw is anyway writing in her notebook and doesn't look thirsty. Ma goes, "Just think about Nixon."

"Nixon? What about Mr. Nixon?"

"He wat'n flexible at all. And look what become of him. Halloween masks is all that's left."

"Well, he did become President of the United States."

"So, what's so great about that? We're talking Balona here."

"That's your final word on debating then, is it, Bapsie? You won't debate."

"Nothing needs to be debated about on. Everybody knows where I stand. I stand for flexibility, just like my Daddy Kon did when he was mayor. Like my Uncle Kosh did when he was judge. Just like my big brother Anson does while he's sheriff. Just like my big brother Syl does while he's being District Attorney of Chaud County." Ma is counting off her influential relatives and pausing between the celebrity names, spelling them out so Mrs. Shaw can get it all down with no mistakes. My ma is actually making quite a speech. If she was completely sober it might be even better.

"All right, so how's about your personal history."

"My personal history. You know about my personal history. So write about it, at least the nice parts. I mean, you wanna make sure you add I was Big Baloney Korndog Kween. That's a big honor nobody will ever forget. You don't need to mention Kenzy or Ginger." She means my dad and my sister. My sister is hiding out in Delta City where she's got a boyfriend who doesn't want to get married and a problem she doesn't want to show off in Balona. "You can mention Joey and Richie. No, better not mention either one. Then you could write more about me."

But it is true about the Korndog Kween part. Back in high school (a place that is known to savvy Balonans as *Big Baloney*) my ma was actually elected Korndog Kween and got to wear her Krown all year. Or she would have worn it all year, except she sat on it around New Years and it is said to have became worst for wear. To this day evil people will say the election was "fixed," but my ma swears it was all on the up and up and that Coach Kork (who was also a student then) had nothing to do with fixing the ballots, no matter what evil people say.

Mrs. Shaw is picking up her things, her green raincoat, her red head scarf, putting away her purple pen and stuff. (I notice all the details because of my training in tradecraft.) My ma speaks, "There's one thing you could promote, though."

Mrs. Shaw stops everything, brings out her notebook and pen, takes off her head scarf, settles back into the couch, raises her eyebrows. Her eyebrows are not startling blonde. They're black, which is probably what makes the blonde part startling. "What's that? What one thing?"

"No debate. But how's about promoting a arm-wrassle championship? I'd be willing to meet the wimp in a public place. Have to have a fair referee, though, and plenty of lights for the TV. You could invite Blip Wufser and the News to come over in his helicopter, sort of share the news with him? And you could have a line open for Buddy Swainhammer to do his talk show over KDC-FM at the same time?" I have never heard my ma make such a long speech sober with so many actual ideas. Of course, she wasn't exactly sober.

"My goodness, Bapsie. Do you mean it?"

"If he won't arm-wrassle, then make it bare knuckles. I could take him bare knuckles, no sweat."

"My goodness, Bapsie. You do mean it!" Mrs. Shaw seems to be excited about being my ma's promoter. She gets herself packed up and is gone in a flash. I bet she goes straight to the *Courier* office to write up her story.

I work up some courage to tell my ma something maybe she doesn't know. "Say, Ma," I go. She is making herself another toddy, this time with ice instead of hot water. She sits down at the kitchen table and slurps the ice, chews on it. She looks at me. Since she has one blue eye and one green eye, when she looks at you it sort of putrefies a guy for a second or two.

"Say Ma what?"

"Mr. Burberry is maybe a spy for MI-6, the British Secret Service and knows secret throws and holts and pins. What I mean is, maybe he was playing possum when you and him arm-wrassled."

"Where'd you hear all that junk?"

"Well, when me and Zack looked into his briefcase. Lots of secret stuff in there. Spy stuff."

"Hah! I bet. Listen, I arm-wrassled lots of guys, and I can tell right away if a guy is trying hard or not. This guy was trying his best. He just cut'n hold a candle to old Lulu here." My ma stroked her arm muscle which she calls "Lulu" for short.

"Hey, Dad," I went, "you going to the office today?"

"I been thinking about it, Joey, uh, Joe." Dad had on his ratty brown bathrobe and his carpet slippers that look like they went through a war in a foxhole." Maybe I'll go on over there if I can find my glasses." It sounded as if Dad might or might not, since it was Saturday, and there's not too much real estate business on Saturday, Dad always says. Sunday, either. It's hard to sell real estate in this market, says Dad, especially without glasses.

I decided I better go on over to Mr. D. H. Carp's Groceries & Sundries where I have a Saturday job waiting for me. I decided to walk and save on gas and the environment. Being late was no problem, since Mr. D. H. Carp is a late sleeper. "Never even spit before noon," is what Mr. D. H. Carp always says about his getting-up habits. I wore my leather bomber jacket that Uncle Kosh gave me, and it and my hair got all wet and plastered down from the fog.

"You're late, Joseph!" went Mr. Piggy Sackworth who I am assistant to in my position as Assistant Chief Bagperson. I put on my green apron and stood by the cash register, watching Balonans drive by on their way to the mall in Delta City.

"I hear your ma is running for mayor."

"Yeh, I guess."

"I hear she's threatening to kick Mr. Burberry's butt."

"Yeh, I guess she could, too."

"Don't tell nobody, but nobody'll vote for her."

"How come's that, Mr. Sackworth?"

"She's a woman. That's how come. Never been a woman mayor here, and never will be. I'll betcha that. But I might vote for her anyways."

"How come's that, Mr. Sackworth?"

"Well, Mr. Burberry's a foreigner. I don't know which would be worst, a woman or a foreigner." Mr. Sackworth wagged his head.

"Well, we'll probably be surprised, either way."

# 17

## Simon Burberry

Except for his towering height and his musculature, Mr. Wong looks like a Chinese. And of course he is a Chinese, possibly Manchurian, because of his square jaw and his high nose.

"No, "I'm not Chinese, Mr. Burberry. I'm Chinese-American, fourth generation American. I'm also a combat veteran of the United States Navy, 16 years service, and I've voted in every national election since I turned 21." Mr. Wong sounded a bit defensive. He served me my *sai minh* perhaps aggressively.

"My ancestors were already over here being persecuted, while your ancestors were busy over in China pillaging and robbing the population. We don't take kindly to persecution in any form any more." I was sure he was correct.

Possibly I should have been more democratic in the manner in which I ordered my lunch. Snapping my fingers to gain his attention, for example. Raising my voice when he appeared not to understand my order. Both of these tactics seem quite reasonably employed by customers seeking the attention of servers who appear challenged by English speech.

As there was no one else at the counter who required his services, I apologized to him and tried to draw him into conversation. "I have some difficulty in being understood, also, Mr. Wong," I remarked, chuckling a bit to take off the chill and not being entirely willing withdraw supinely. An Englishman has his pride.

"Hey, Mr. Burberry, I have no difficulty being understood. With foreigners, I just holler at 'em." His deep voice was raised as he said this. "And there's something else to keep in mind." He lifted his eyebrows, about to impart something of great moment. "My great-grandpa used to tell me that in the Old Country when loudmouth arrogant foreigners snapped their fingers at you, as if you were a dog, and you were serving, well, all you had to do was quietly spit in their soup before you placed it on the table. Made you feel a whole lot better!"

I suspect that Mr. Wong may have been teasing, for he did chuckle and twinkle, finally. Without meaning to, I did glance down at my *sai minh* with some suspicion. He laughed again.

"Well, Mr. Wong, although you are of the fourth-generation, perhaps you may know of a reliable herbalist."

"Oh, you got some troubles? Like maybe voice problems? Swollen head? That sort of thing?"

"I have a need to have an herbal prescription refilled. Mr. Vibrissa doesn't do herbs, he claims."

"Well, that's not what I hear!" Mr. Wong twinkled again.

"Do you in fact know of such a place?"

"Sure. Everybody knows Wong's. Pacific Avenue in Delta City. North past C4 and on the right-hand side of the street as you're going toward Lodi."

"Ah. A relative."

"No relation. Plenty of Wongs."

"But no two Wongs make a white!" I raise my voice in laughter, jar my bowl with my enthusiastic forearm. Mr. Wong does not grasp the humour, adjusts the bowl so that it is closer to me. I resume my meal.

Mr. Wong leans on the counter before me, his large knuckles showing prominently. "That's the kind of joke that good friends might make if they grew up in Balona and dit'n have much taste. A stranger in town who's supposed to have some class wut'n make such a joke. Specially one who's got to suck up to the voters if he's gonna be mayor." He walks back into the kitchen. I have been politically incorrect. Worse, I have been impertinent and perceived as unfriendly. I shall find a way to redeem myself with Mr. Wong.

Perhaps it is that Mother Crinkle has upset me with her harping accusingly that her friend with the disturbing red wig, Ms Splinters, is not answering her telephone. Mother Crinkle left home leaning on her brolly shortly after breakfast and fortunately had not returned in time to prepare my lunch. It was necessary for me to venture out for the noonday meal. Mr. Wong will serve korndogs at his Peking Peek-Inn, but the item is noted on the menu as orderable on "special request only." I was not about to submit a special request!

But my breakfast remained heavy in my abdomen all morning while I worked on the new box. The gravel in my socks this morning was no help, either. I am determined to get to the Delta City Wong establishment as soon after lunch as possible.

The bright spot in my week, in addition to the cheerful reception I got at the Solidarity breakfast are the generally happy greetings I receive on the street from average Balonans. And I am enjoying the courting behavior of Mr. Sam Joe Sly. I have even enjoyed Mr. Sly's leaps of logic and his assumptions about my background, interests, and abilities.

Mr. Sly ("Hey, call me Sam Joe, Simon") has departed Balona "for a coupla days, Simon. Las Vegas calls!" Mr. Sly terms himself a keen judge of horseflesh. "When I seen you, Simon, I says to myself, Sam Joe, here is a guy gonna make us both a pisspot of money." Sam Joe slapped me on the back, squeezed my bicep, both Balona indicators of eternal friendship.

"I am pleased to think you may be right."

"So, I'm gonna propose you come into binnis with me. Full partner. Salary plus bonuses and perks. Alls you need is a little capital investment—a few thou is all—to show good faith. I hear you got plenty, so a few thou won't make a dent in your stash, right?" Sam Joe snorted, catarrh-wise, and almost looked me in the eye. He does have an outside squint which makes eye contact a challenge. "You got a good stash of cash, right?"

"I have funds, yes. What would my duties be, please?"

"Well, I been thinking about that and, y'know, it got me thinking about fish and chips."

"Ah."

"Yeh. That's what you people eat on, right? Fish and chips. Got a fish and chips place on every corner?"

"Almost."

"Yeh. Well, I was thinking what would go good with fish and chips over there, something you guys don't have. Y'know?"

"Something we don't have."

"Yeh. King Korndogs. A little King Korndog shop right next to your fish and chips shops. Make your diet more healthy, with vitamins, not to say flavour." Sam Joe cleared his nasal passages. "The big deal that made me think of you is, you got a real gift of gab. So you could start right in figuring out how we're gonna get King Korndog started over there where we can improve the health of the country. With a name like *King* Korndog, we'll be right there on the ground floor when the old lady dies off, y'know?"

Sam Joe is surely alluding to the Queen. Perhaps he is unaware of the durable genes of our old Queen Mum.

"Also we're expecting the inspectors to come this next week, right? Right? Get the picture here?"

"How do I begin helping you—helping *us*—make money?"

"Hey, you got the picture! So, first thing is, you are gonna help us not get fined. That's how. So, what you do is just greet those guys. Feed 'em a spiel, like. Pour coffee. Pour 'em tea and crumpets! Live it up. Keep 'em in the office. Make my excuses. Like, tell 'em I'm at the Better Health for California Children Conference down in Hollywood."

"My word, is that a fact!"

"No, no, I should say not! That's just a way of getting 'em to understand my fine desire to do good works. Actually, I'm gonna be in Las Vegas, like I said. Gonna fly out of Delta City. Got my own Cessna, y'know. You will be the official greeter and entertainer, right? Right?"

"If you believe I might be adequate for your purposes."

"Hey, I already said. You got the style. You, guy, are perfect for my purposes. Our purposes, partner. You just be flexible and keep the inspectors out of the plant. That's all. You and me'll work out our details later. So, when do you put it on the line?"

"Pardon?"

"When do I get your deposit?"

"Oh. Well, I could manage a few thousand here and now." I opened my case and withdrew several packets of bills and, given the likelihood of gaining more income shortly, not bothering to count them. I placed them on Sam Joe's desk. "And what is the money for, or is that none of my business?"

Sam Joe licked his lips. "Well, I never gamble with my own cash, man. Everybody knows that. Oh, you mean what do *you* get out of this? Yeh, sure. Well, you get the keys to the place. You can play with any of the toys out there. Just remember they're dangerous and be sure you don't fall in!" Sam Joe bent over almost double in mirth. "And—see, I do know my horseflesh—I already ordered your binnis cards. They'll be right here on the desk in a coupla days, before the inspectors, so you can pass 'em around."

I now had my own desk, my own slicker, my own gumboots, and my own keys to King Korndog's *sanctum sanctorum*. Astonishing how bounteously one may be served by fate.

Hardly had Sam Joe departed than I donned slicker and gumboots and made my first official tour as partner. The word had been spread even before my arrival. Horseflesh knowledge again. Workers saluted. A forklift operator blew his horn several times and waved. Cows mooed movingly. The chopper hopper operator dipped and turned his platform gracefully, raised his cigar above his control panel, allowing one of his legs to dangle tantalizingly over the vat. At the end of my tour a baker offered me a fresh hot product which I smilingly refused.

It felt good to be recognized as a productive person, a man of responsibility and good character. A candidate.

Mr. Wong returned, took my bowl and spoon, and wiped condensation from the counter. He used his wiping cloth with considerable expertise. "I'll wager you were an expert cook in the navy, Mr. Wong."

"I was mostly a shore patrolman, a petty officer first class, Mr. Burberry."

Wrong surmise.

After I received detailed directions from Mr. Wong as to the location of Wong's, I at last found my missing keys and was on the way to Delta City in no time at all. This time my case was safely on the seat beside me. The fog had lifted and under the cover of gray clouds the countryside appeared much like East Anglia.

I drove carefully this time, staying on the proper side of the road, making signals according to the instructions in the Vehicle Code, driving over a kerb only once. The windscreen was still spotted with the corpses of small insects. I would need to clean it for the return trip. At the moment my attention was focused on getting through Delta City, finding Wong's and refilling my prescription.

Time was running out.

Wong's was as easy to find as Mr. Wong had described it. I parked, locked the vehicle and with case in hand, entered the dim interior. A man of Asian appearance raised his head from work at the counter.

"Mr. Wong, I presume."

"Nope. Name's Jack Lee."

Ah. Perhaps another of the fourth-generation. I explained my predicament, brought out my capsule container, held the green capsule up for his inspection.

"Well, what is this, a health food supplement?"

"I believe it is, mm, an anodyne and a relaxant."

"Oh, we have all sorts of stuff to relax you. Zonk you right out." Perhaps Mr. Jack Lee was fifth-generation.

"For homeostatsis I require the specific contents of this capsule. I am used to these contents and this dosage. If I don't have these capsules I suffer gravely. Gravely."

"Well, let's take a look-see." Mr. Jack Lee popped open the capsule, sniffed at it. Frowned. "This is a weird one, all right. You got this from a Chinese herbalist?"

"Doctor Schimpf was Hindu-influenced."

"Oh, well. Hindu. That's a whole new ballgame. We don't stock stuff by Hindu name, y'know."

"I thought this establishment's being herbal you would be able to recognize herbal contents."

"I can get maybe close. Tell you what, I'll find some nice agreeable ingredients, grind 'em up nice, probably smell a lot like this, and then you try it out. If it works, fine. If not, it won't cost you all that much and we could try something else. Okay?"

What choice did I have. I could feel intimations of trembling approaching. But I was aware of an odd circumstance. The hints I felt were not as pronounced as those I experienced several days ago. During the intervening days something must have occurred in my subconscious to release my tensions. I wonder what it could have been. Perhaps it was visiting King Korndog and becoming an instant partner. Or my visits to the plant. Perhaps it has been my diet. Perhaps it is the prospect of elective office. Perhaps it is simply a Balona Phenomenon.

These new substitute capsules may have the necessary beneficial effect.

Mr. Jack Lee hastened after me and at the car handed me my case, which in my funk I had forgotten. Perhaps that is also a Balona Phenomenon. I must watch my step.

# 18
### Joseph Oliver Kuhl

Me and Zack were at the Balona Dump recently. The dump is a place where you pay a dollar to old Lud Langsam and maybe you can find all sorts of treasures. February is the best time to visit the dump, since even though it's pretty damp and gooey, at least it doesn't smell now the way it usually smells. You don't want to go near the dump in the summer, except it is a fact that I have found really good stuff there in summer, since nobody else is brave enough to attempt a search under those circumstances.

We had our dumpsticks with us, of course. Your dumpstick is the device authentic Balona guys use to poke around with, lift stuff up with, and generally explore with. Some Balona guys take great pride in their dumpsticks, treating them with the same kind of care that guys in other places ravish on their cars. I don't treat my dumpstick like it was a holy thing like a car. Mine is a plain dumpstick, no ornaments, no paint or varnish on it, just a good point on it.

On the other hand, Zack's dumpstick is custom, with a clothes-hanging hook he's screwed onto the working end. It's actually pretty effective with that hook on it, but I wouldn't mention that to him since a compliment would just bloat up his head more while I'm still trying to figure out a way to take him down a peg or two.

We were also wearing our rubber boots, of course. Zack was wearing his yellow slicker and I had my brown leather bomber jacket on, since it was a chilly afternoon and the sun was going down fast. We were both wearing our fashionable black knit terrorist caps to keep the fog off. These are the kind you can pull down over your face that have round red holes for your eyes and your mouth. You can really scare little kids and old folks with these caps, too, if you're still into that sort of thing, which even Zack isn't any more.

While poking around, me and Zack were having a sort of philosophical discussion, which is what you better do when dump-searching if you're not finding anything interesting, or else you might get overcome by the environment. We had been talking about Mr. Burberry.

Everybody's talking about Mr. Burberry. Not only about the neat boxes he makes and about how suave he is and about how flexible he likely will be when he gets to be Mayor of Balona (if he can whip my ma). But also about the amazing fact that Mrs. Bena Splinters was so suddenly took up with his style that she turned over all her property and bank accounts and cash to him before she left town to join her son in Montana.

Her son Card, the guy who supposedly disappeared from his job at King Korndog, is not missing after all. He finally revealed that he is somewhere in Montana, doing well, has a good job, and misses his mother. There were tears in lots of Balona female eyes to hear that part about missing his mother, since Balona guys don't usually mention stuff like that on postcards. It just goes to show how, when you move to Montana, you would probably go soft.

Old Mrs. Splinters said on the postcard she wrote to Zack's dad that since Mr. Burberry is so nice, and since old Card is now so successful and rich up there in Montana, then it's only fair that a nice newcomer like Mr. Burberry should get the benefit of her estate in order to make him feel welcome.

"That dut'n sound to me like a true Balona person would do that. You ever hear of an old-time Balona person doing something like that? I wonder how come everybody believes all that?" If Zack wasn't a high school youth he would be known at Chaud County Community College as a cynic, which is a guy that doesn't believe anything you tell him. "I mean, all that stuff people are talking about came out of my dad."

"No, Zack. Card sent his ma all those postcards telling her the good news. And then when Card's ma left town, she sent a bunch of postcards telling everybody how happy she is."

"Not exactly to everybody, Joe. All the postcards got sent to Da."

"Well, I hear they were all good old Balona postcards, so you know they're authentic."

"Joe, all the postcards got sent to Da. You hear what I'm saying?" What Zack is saying is that Uncle Kenworth Burnross is the one who has revealed all these details about old Mrs. Splinters and her son Card and Mr. Burberry.

"Well, of course, Young Zack. What I mean is, if you was in Criminal Justice you would know that's only natural. Uncle

Kenworth is Mr. Burberry's lawyer. He is Mrs. Splinters's lawyer, too, I guess, since he knows all about her son and her private binnis. So what if it came out of your dad? So what? Wut'n you expect that?"

"Well, don't mention I said it, but as you may well know Da can't remember one day from another, much less who is his client. But, yeh, he's Mr. Burberry's lawyer all right. Da was bragging about it at breakfast one day last week. Said he was gonna make a pile of money to send me to Harvard or Oxford with."

Zack is always talking about going to college when he isn't even out of high school yet, an unusual trope for a Balona guy. He also badmouths his dad a lot, even though his dad is saving up to send his kid to Harvard or Oxford. This is not unusual for a Balona guy, but me badmouthing my dad is something I stopped doing quite a while ago, when I finally grew up and realized that my dad was my actual dad, the only one I would ever have. And the guy who gave me my *sang froyd* and my name. And also my friend who would give me the shirt off of his back if he had one. Also, that my dad is sort of a sad guy who needs me hanging around to cheer him up with talk about my future plans, clients, et cetera.

"Hey, lookey here!" Zack had snagged an object with his dumpstick. It was a Runcibles in the Mall shopping bag. He held it out for us to take a look.

"It looks like it's in good shape. No gunk on it at all. Must be a newcomer to the dump." We both laughed at my humor.

Zack drew the thing near and peeked into it. "Aw, honk! It's just got clothes and stuff in it."

"Well, let's give it a evidentiary examination." I often use Criminal Justice terminology, just to get used to using it. Anyway, we found a sort of clean dry place and dumped out the bag.

Zack sounded grouchy. "Well, honk. This stuff shut've gotten taken to the St. Vincent de Paul. It's got no holes or anything. Lookey here: a raincoat, no holes. A pair of galoshes, no holes. Headscarf or big hanky. Some homeless fat person would like to have this stuff. Yeh, your ma would go for this thing, I bet." He held up the object, shook it out.

"Hey, it's a, a, a muumuu! I'll be daggone! You're right about the holiness. No hole at all, see? Yeh, and it looks huge enough, so I bet my ma would go for it. It's at least clean-looking. Not like her yellow one with the maplenut ice cream stains." I sniffed at it. "It does smell a little rich."

"Consider where we found it. Anyways, my ma wut'n wear such a thing. Wut'n wear any of this stuff, in fact. Mummy's a fashion-place, all right."

Zack will badmouth his ma, too, even though she makes him those gourmet sandwiches and always treats him like he was coming down with a famous disease. I will badmouth my ma, but only because she deserves it. And only if she can't hear me. In this case I was deciding to make her a gift. I decided then and there I wouldn't tell her where I got it.

"I wonder who would throw away good stuff like this."

"Well, don't worry about it, Joe. You can take the whole kit and kaboodle home as a gift to A'nt Bapsie. Tell her you've turned over a new leaf from now on. Maybe she'll finally give you an allowance and you can quit your job at Mr. D. H. Carp's Groceries & Sundries." Zack smirked one-sided, like he knew that would never happen.

I have to think of a way to take him down a peg or two. But I grabbed up the shopping bag full of good stuff and held it on the side away from Lud as we tramped out of the dump. I did the concealment trope since Lud might have taken the bag back to try to sell it at the Delta City fleamarket, which is his usual thing about good stuff. The Runcibles shopping bag just happened to escape his eagle eye. My good luck.

When I got home, first thing I took the bag up to my room and dumped it onto my bed so as to examine the evidence more closely. The galoshes were too small for my ma's feet. Anyway, my ma goes barefoot most of the time, since she believes that shoes give athlete's foot.

The huge colored hanky I decided to keep for myself, since maybe I could use it as a Christmas or birthday gift for Claire or Willow or Millie. Even though Claire is always hanging out with Jack Ordway and Willow nowadays gives me nothing but chilly glances, and Millie is all hung up on Sal Shaw. There's always Patella, but if I gave her a nice huge colored hanky like this, she would take it personal.

The raincoat I folded up to take downstairs when nobody was looking and hang it on a nail in our new garage for the use of guests and my dad when he gets thrown out of the house in rainy weather.

The muumuu I waved around for a while, trying to get the smell out, since it reminded you of the perfume counter at

Runcibles in the Mall over in Delta City. I looked in my closet and found the box my Christmas underwear came in. I always get underwear for Christmas, and I always save the box. I have a closet full of underwear boxes.

The muumuu fit in the box just right, even without froo-froo paper to fold it up in. I figured my ma would be so surprised to get a gift from me that she wouldn't notice it didn't come all wrapped up nice.

And she was. I waited until we'd finished our Peking Peek-Inn takeout meal of chop suey and egg rolls. Mr. Wong calls his chop suey *chow mein*, but it's all the same to me. I eat what I get, which is a lesson my ma taught us all a long time ago.

Me and Dad ate up our chop suey in a real hurry, him because he thinks maybe Mr. Burberry is going to let Dad in on a house sale, he says.

"Mr. Burberry come by today when me and Killer was taking our afternoon nap at Frings Bowls. He sat right down in the booth with us, like a regular Balona guy. Had coffee. Bought me a cup, too." Dad looked proud to be associating with the likes of Mr. Burberry, a classy guy. "Maybe he'll call pretty soon."

"So, Dad. Mr. Burberrry's gonna buy a house from you?"

Dad looked sad right away. He burped and mentioned, "Well, no. He said about how that now he had come into some real estate, he would be looking for a way to make it pay off. That's what he actually said. So I went that I would be happy to handle the binnis end for him, and he sort of went how he'd think about it."

Ma horned in. "Mr. Burberry is gonna sell off Bena Splinters's place that he just got from her? Nerve on the guy."

"Well, Baps, honey, Mr. Burberry cut'n use a big house like that with just one guy living in it. Besides, if I sell it, it'll mean a nice commission."

"Ha!" was all my ma said, but the way she said it was enough to make my dad sad again, and he excused himself and went into the living room to sit in his chair and look down at the carpet and rub his eyes.

If I ever get married, it won't be to somebody who gets a kick out of making me sad. So I decided that was a good as time as any to present my present. Sort of suck up to my ma. Zack could possibly be right about the allowance. I reached under the table and pulled out the box, handed it across to my ma. "Here is a token of my self-esteem, Ma, since it's just the right color for your complexion, eksedra. I picked it out myself." Which was the truth, if you didn't examine the truth too close.

"What the *diddly-blonk*!" Ma snatched the cover off the box with one hand and whipped the muumuu out with the other. "I'll be *dingly-booped*! This is a present? From you, Joey? Well, I never. Well, I'll just go try it on. See if it fits." So she went off to the downstairs bathroom and was in there for a while, probably looking at herself in the mirror. It sounded like she was pleased.

She opened the bathroom door. She had actually combed her hair and stood there like a huge Korndog Kween (without the Krown, of course). "Yeh. It fits all right, the way a muumuu will fit no matter what. Well, Joey. I just don't know what to say. Lem'me give you a hug!" When she marched towards me I took off up the stairs and hid in my room. She being cheerful and actually saying thanks-a-lot was one thing. A hug would be too much for one day.

# 19
## Simon Burberry

Assassins. Perhaps. Perhaps not.

The new capsules seem to be effective. Although my trembling and fantastic thoughts are present, they appear to be declining. I am sleeping more soundly than in many a month. I am entertaining the notion that perhaps the "assassins" pursuing me are instead only incompetent "messengers." This estimate seems valid, despite the allegation that Madog was carrying a replica Walther PPK.

Madog's likely view, widely held in the UK, is that the United States, especially the Western States, are an untamed and violent place not greatly advanced from Wild West days. Such might provide the rationale for his pilfering my PPK from the secret storage in the hayloft of the stables. I had designed the location so that, if discovered, the display of contents might convince the pilferer that he had found the complete treasure. He would necessarily have had to have reason to search more diligently. Had he done so, he might also have discovered several of my first boxes, in which case the outcome might be even less pleasant.

The troubling question remains: Why have those two fellows come to this country with their accusations? If they have not sought to murder me at someone's behest or out of simple envy, then why are they here laboring to destroy my faultless reputation?

Perhaps it is Silas Blade who has put them up to this. But Blade has been out of sight these many days. I do not want to raise Blade simply to enable discovery of the answer to these questions.

I do wish I could see dear Mum again. She is so frequently in my thoughts. I was recalling only yesterday, while walking the plant floor and drawing the usual salutes from my adoring employees, how happy I was as a child. It was Mum who steered me in the direction of service, a choice I have only fleetingly deplored, and then only because of the regrettable incident accompanying the disappearance of Lady Demelza. Mr. Tudwick's frustration followed at once by his anger were perhaps understandable, but his pointing in my direction was ungrounded, unjustified. My unannounced leaving then precipitated immediate need, although the celerity with which I departed did cast unwarranted suspicion that it was I who had something to do with Lady Demelza's continuing absence from Tudwick Hall (hated name). Yes, that was thoughtless haste.

Of course, it is conceivable that Blade may have had something to do with that disappearance, but I prefer not to think about that. I have been thinking instead of my Arcadian childhood, of a warm kitchen, rain sounding on the slates, of Mum's beneficent hovering alternating with the occasional and unexpected severe beating, all in a green, moist, and pleasant land. Of course, the pleasant land also held unpleasantness, persistent memories such as the black dog's devouring my dear pet Ginzo, his head and little feet and other bloody remains left on the doorstep. And the cat that was somehow drowned in my bath, a mystery to this day. And the pigeon that....I must cleanse my mind of these things.

I was recalling more and varied pleasant thoughts of home when summoned by telephone to another interview by young Patella Sackworth, this time at the office of the Balona *Courier*, the place where my case was recovered. The young woman is persistent in her efforts to celebrate me in the press. Now that my location appears to be common knowledge, and seemingly of no consequence to any agency, I am re-thinking the need for anonymity.

"I wut've liked to go on over to your place, Mr. Burberry, and, like, do our thing over there, but Mrs. Shaw and Grandpa both said it wat'n, like, proper for a pretty young virgin-type girl to be locked up alone, like, with a virile handsome older man with a mustache. So that's why you got to come on over here."

I checked my mustache as well as my wig to ensure the match of color. I donned my new cashmere for the interview. It is a fawn color and of splended fit, thanks to the tailor at Runcibles in the Mall, a Delta City establishment.

"You a foreigner?" the tailor had inquired.

"English." I was determined to be civil.

"Yeh. I come from Egypt, so I know English. French, too."

I did not reveal that I am fluent in that language, and seven others. And that I am a superb shot with any imaginable firearm, and competent with throwing stars and knives. And that my virtual SAS training has equipped me superbly for adventuring by land, sea, or air. I did not deign to show him my badge and simulated credentials. The fellow did a creditable job with the jacket, but there was no reason to impress an obvious social inferior. So I controlled my inclination to do so.

The tailor was competent and voluble, but surly as well, a trait that I have discovered is common among persons engaged in that craft. To complement the fawn, I chose a mauve silk shirt to wear with my fine dark paisley ascot, charcoal trousers, and the burgundy boots that take such a fine high polish. Typical Balonans would not call them *boots*. They would point and say, unimaginatively and undiscriminatingly, *"yer shoes there."* But if I am to triumph in the upcoming election, I must train myself to demonstrate that I hold all Balonans in high esteem. That is, I must be *flexible*.

I would have shown attentiveness and great care in the selection of attire for Mr. Tudwick, had that inferior fat little fellow not so boldly squinted his eyes at me and pursed his pouty lips and shaken his head. He would have benefited from wearing navy or charcoal or black instead of his *gauche* checked coat and white socks on all occasions.

Of course, I was loyal retainer to Lady Demelza alone, not a lowly manservant, and he could not stand her defence of my presence, though she had named the mansion in his honour. Had she not insisted on wearing the red wig, had I been more faithful in taking my capsules, had the weather been cooler and the Bentley more tractable, had I not failed to remove the box from the boot, had Blade not suddenly appeared, had we not ventured so close to Pascoe's....Well, it is of little value to re-live the past.

The sky is cloudy today, and the breeze is brisk, but the feel of the air on the skin is cool, not cold. I shall walk to my appointment, taking my brolly as insurance against the weather.

"Oo, you look so handsome. Dut'n he look handsome, Bellona?" My amanuensis squealed embarrassingly, but I felt warmly supported nevertheless, much as my dear "Natasha" would squeal whenever she beheld me, particularly at that final occasion when she made the special effort to impress me. An error on her part—but then, it is one of life's great truths that one must learn to live, however briefly thereafter, with one's mistakes.

Patella Euphella held some sheets of yellow paper on high. "See here, Mr. Burberry. I got a column about you all ready to pass off to Grandpa!"

"I take it I have opportunity to contest the contents?" I managed to show my teeth, all the while worrying that in the absence of the good brushing that in my haste I forgot to accomplish, my incisors might be displaying part of my lunch. Placing my hand over my mouth, I began to work on the teeth with my tongue and facial muscles.

"Hey, you got something wrong with your throat or tooth there? You getting a tooth problem?" This from Mr. Patrick Preene, watching from across the room. It is very like the Balona character to comment on other such personal matters as the variety of sounds associated with the digestive processes, the wheezing of nasal passages, hair in and about orifices, organic odors, the detritis on one's shoulders, et cetera.

"No, not at all." *A well-told lie clears the head.*

I have created an apothegm, but of course, I am unable to use it at this time.

"You get to look at what I've, like, written here, Mr. Burberry, uh, Simon, but Grandpa always has to, like, have the last word."

Patella has typed out her column as it might appear unedited in the next issue of the *Courier*.

Patella's Patter
by Patella Euphella Sackworth

Tall, suave, handsome Mr. Simon Burberry, lately of England but now a proud resident of Balona, is here in town sort of by accident. Mr. Burberry, in his velvet tones coming out from under a smooth mustache on a tannish face, made it clear that he has found Balona to be "a lovely place."

"I have found Balona to be a lovely place," is what the stylish Englishman mentioned to this reporter during our private one-on-one interview just this week.

Mr. Burberry has got beaver-brown eyes, says Mrs. Billa Crinkle, Mr. Burberry's landlady, where the suave Englishman lives with her in her house on Fourth Street. This reporter can confirm that fact, too, from her close observation over coffee with the handsome Englishman.

"Yes, I am from England," he said.

Mr. Burberry, a candidate for Mayor of Balona, said only yesterday that he thought Balonans are "very nice people who are polite and fine people."

Mr. Burberry, who has become a member of Solidarity already is also a new partner in King Korndog Inkorporated, a well-known Balona firm with world-wide implications.

"I am glad I found this place. Balona has charms to sooth the savage breast," mentioned Mr. Burberry to this reporter recently.

# # #

Miss Patella and Mr. Patrick Preene examined my face for signs of approval or disapproval.

"I haven't edited it yet," said Mr. Preene, "but then, it dut'n seem to need much editing." He looked appreciatively at his granddaughter.

"I wrote it so's it, like, wut'n need editing, Grandpa, since I know you don't like to, like, do much editing. But what do you think, Simon?"

"You should address our next mayor as Mr. Burberry, Patella. It's not nice for a young woman to call a mature man by his first name. It's, uh, forward."

"Simon dut'n mind, do you, Simon?"

I raised my shoulders and my eyebrows and twinkled quietly, not wishing to disagree with either party. "Perhaps I shall begin referring to Miss Patella as Patella Euphella."

Miss Patella Euphella did not twinkle at this essay in humour. "It's not wrong, but it's my professional name. It's not very friendly to say it that way, Simon."

The argument remained unresolved, for at that moment, Mrs. Shaw, the blonde woman with the black eyebrows, swept into the office, breathless. "Guess what! The sheriff has let Mr. Blight go. Says he's got no case against him. Says nobody in town would admit to seeing him ride the mower to Billa Crinkle's house. Says if we can tolerate one Englishman in Balona, we can tolerate another."

I felt a definite chill at the news. "Can you interpret that for me, Mrs. Shaw? That is, does the sheriff mean to return Mr. Blight to Balona?"

"That's it, all right. Constable Cod's probably letting him out of the car at this very moment." Mrs. Shaw went to the window, perhaps to verify her conjecture.

I decided to *grab the korndog by the collar*, (as Balonans say), and have it out with Blight at once. "I shall face him and discover the truth," I announced. Mrs. Shaw and Miss Patella both took out their notebooks and began writing.

Mr. Preene remarked, "I guess we got a good lead story for the next edition." He glanced at Miss Patella. "It might make for better reading than what you got for me there, Patella."

The rejection did not at once register with Miss Patella who was busy writing. I am sure she was not happy that her column would not grace the front page of the next edition of the *Courier*, but I did not witness her response, as I was already out the door and on my way to the constable's office where I was sure I might find Blight.

# 20
### Joseph Oliver Kuhl

I was standing at the end of the counter at Mr. D. H. Carp's Groceries & Sundries, sort of looking out the window into the rain, when three things happened all at once—four or five things if you count Mr. Burberry.

All our customers were probably home watching TV or napping, so they were not one of the things. Mr. D. H. Carp was in his office with his feet up on his desk looking at a buff-guy magazine which he had disguised inside a nature magazine. Mr. Carp may be a little bent. Mr. Sackworth was taking his fifth potty break of the morning. Neither of those guys are in my count. I had on my green apron and was chewing on some jerky, a food I like if I don't think about where it came from. That's not one of the things, either.

The things were: Down the street a little ways, Cod pulled up in his car in front of his office. He had a passenger who got out first. It was Mr. Blight, wearing a cap and looking none the worst for his stay in Uncle Anson's jail over in Delta City. And then the piece of resistance came: Mr. Burberry in his black hat and trenchcoat and black umbrella came whipping around the corner making for Cod's office.

Cod's office is not all that big a place, especially when you get Cod into it. Cod's got all his snack-making equipment laid out in there, including his microwave, his popcorn machine, his coffee maker, his fridge, et cetera. It's the back room with the chains on the wall where his temporary "guests" are stashed. Right at present, Cod's got no guests back there.

I wondered how come Mr. Blight was associating with Cod, since Cod was known to have been sort of rude to Mr. Blight, twisting his arm and chaining him up and sort of starving him. But right away I figured it must be the Stockholm Syndrome at work on the guy, which I just learned about in Criminal Justice.

The Stockholm Syndrome is where, after a guy has been beat on for a while, he starts to enjoy it and comes to like the guy beating on him. I probably have acquired the Stockholm Syndrome from my ma beating up on me. It actually doesn't work on me the way Mr. Dainty told us yesterday, since I still don't particularly like my ma or enjoy she beating on me.

Since Mr. Carp had now nodded off into the arms of Murphy and Mr. Sackworth was still in the john, there was no reason except the job for me to stay on duty. So I slipped across the street, first having forgot to take off my apron. The guys looked surprised when I entered Cod's office. Nobody even said hello.

Cod was plopped in his beat-up chair and Mr. Blight and Mr. Burberry were sitting on the folding chairs Cod's got there. The chairs are especially uncomfortable so he never has to entertain visitors for very long.

"I'm just looking for some possible material for my next *Courier* column, so I'll just lurk here by the door while you guys go on about your binnis." I thought my explanation was pretty suave. None of them said anything, just kept looking at each other, sort of ignoring me.

Mr. Blight kept looking at Mr. Burberry. He was frowning and scratching his head under his brown cap which he hadn't taken off. The cap was the flat cloth kind you see guys wear in old movies, not the kind with a logo for *King Korndog* or *Mudville Nine* on it that guys around here wear backwards to show how suave they are. Mr. Blight is short, skinny, black-haired, sort of twisted looking. He has warts on his face and needed a shave. He moved his scratching fingers around under the cap, probably to get at the best itches. He kept on frowning. Mr. Burberry just sat there and let Mr. Blight look at him. Finally Mr. Blight said something.

"Who're you, sir?" is what he said. A saying that sort of surprised me, since I was under the impression he knew Mr. Burberry since he had accused Mr. Burberry of something.

"Simon Burberry, my good man. Simon Burberry."

"You're not Silas Blade." It sounded like Mr. Blight was accusing Mr. Burberry.

"As I just said, I am Simon Burberry. I am interested in why you were harassing me with the lawn mowing machine and making unjustifiable accusations of some sort." Mr. Burberry took off his hat and placed it over one knee. He smoothed his hair and his mustache, looked suave, put his hat on Cod's desk corner, crossed his legs, dangled his shiny shoe, turned it this way and that, admiring it sort of.

"Well, sir, that's betwixt me and Mr. Blade. I was after Mr. Blade. We thought sure you was Silas Blade when we heard there was an Englishman just come here. A friend told me he might be around these parts and I should keep looking whilst he went elsewheres."

"'We,' you said. 'A friend.'"

"An associate, you might say, sir. A Mr. Madog. Me and him, we come over together, looking for Mr. Blade."

"Must have been an important mission for the two of you to make such a long trip to find the fellow." Mr. Burberry sounded like he was using tradecraft interrogation methods straight out of the UITS manual. I was impressed with his style.

"We had news for him, sir, and maybe a deal to make, y'know."

"I understood you were accusing him of criminal activity."

"That was to get the law's help in flushing him out, you might say."

"So, there's no crime this fellow Blade is accused of?"

"Ah, as to that. Who knows? We, me and Madog, we got a deal for him to consider. So if you know where he went, maybe you could give us a clue?"

"Well, I believe that Silas Blade was here briefly and has now departed this area. Probably in Canada or Argentina or Thailand by this time."

"Oh, that's too bad." Mr. Blight looked at his shoes, which were brown leather and not all that clean. "I don't think I got enough money left to keep on looking for him. I don't know that I got enough money to get back to home."

"Perhaps Mr. Madog will return."

"Well, sir, I don't know. We split up so as to make our search more effective, you might say, but I don't know now." Mr. Blight wagged his head and shuffled his shoes. A sad fellow who just heard bad news.

Cod sat there eating popcorn out of a huge brown bag. He made noises every once in a while, but they were mostly wheezing and digestive-type noises. He didn't seem interested in the conversation.

Mr. Blight went, "But you sound like Mr. Blade. You know? You sound a lot like him. Except that Mr. Blade's got blue eyes and a yellow mustache and is bald, you sound just like him. Amazing. Maybe you're a relation?"

Mr. Burberry smiled, crinkled his eyes and smiled.

Mr. Blight had an accent, but different than Mr. Burberry's. Not so refined. Mr. Blight's accent seemed to stay right behind his teeth. Mr. Burberry's was mostly in his nose.

Mr. Burberry sat very still, except for the dangling shoe. He held his head up, along with one eyebrow. Mr. Blight wiggled on his chair, wringing his hands and giving the impression he had a flea in his shorts. He kept looking at the floor and then back at Mr. Burberry.

Mr. Blight went on frowning. "I don't know," he groaned. "You sure you're not Mr. Blade?"

Mr. Burberry threw back his head and laughed a *ha ha ha* in his nose. "I've been Simon Burberry all my life, my good man."

"Well, he even laughs like Mr. Blade." Mr. Blight directed this comment at Cod, who only raised his eyebrows and burped.

I felt I had to support Mr. Burberry who was getting kind of insulted here. I went, "This is Mr. Burberry, all right. I can guarantee that."

Mr. Burberry twinkled at me and nodded his approval of how I had entered the conversation just in time to show my friendship for a guy who just might give me a good recommendation to the Queen some day. He turned to Mr. Blight. "As you seem to be short of cash, Mr. Blight, perhaps we could do one another a small favor, and we might both benefit."

"How so, sir?"

"I have a property that is vacant at the moment, and if you were to reside there temporarily, I would be happy to compensate you for your trouble. I wish to ensure that the house appears to be occupied so as to discourage vandals and thieves. You would thus have a pleasant place to stay, and some pounds in your pocket besides."

Mr. Burberry was surely talking about Mrs. Splinters's place, where Mr. Burberry has inherited it but is still living at Mrs. Crinkle's.

"Well, that is kind of you, indeed, sir."

"Just helping a fellow countryman. And I could show you around Balona's wonderful chief business in which I am a partner."

"What business might that be, sir? A bank? A mine?"

"Ha ha ha. No, my good man, it's King Korndog Inkorporated, a magical place with an extraordinary product." Mr. Burberry uncrossed his leg and slapped his thigh. "By Jove! Let's have a korndog right now, all of us! Frank's is practically next door. You shall all be my guests!"

"Hey," went Cod, sort of waking up. "I'll go for that, only I'm hooked on Franksburgers, y'know. Hope you don't mind, since you're paying for it." Cod always tries to make sure he isn't the one who pays for the Franksburgers.

"Mr. Blight here will surely enjoy a korndog or two. Much improved over a sausage roll or a toad-in-the-hole, Mr. Blight, especially with the fine local sauce. And young Mr. Kuhl may join us."

"Hey, all right!" I went, and led the group to an early lunch.

"Mr. Backhouse, are your korndogs frozen or fresh?"

"Delivered fresh from the Kastle Keep this morning, Mr. Burberry!"

I had two korndogs and Frank's version of a Hires, a drink which usually has got a lot of fizz, but at Frank's it's sort of flat. Mr. Burberry had a Franksburger which he improved by putting some korndog sauce on it, an act that seemed to offend Frank, but which old Cod tried, too, on both of his Franksburgers.

Mr. Blight had two korndogs, the first one without sauce, the next one with. He made *umming* noises while he ate, turning and looking at each of us and smirking with his mouth mostly open so you could see the korndogs getting sloshed up inside there.

"It's sure a surprise finding a bloke what reminds me of Mr. Blade so much. I guess you're sure you're no relation. But it's amazing." Mr. Blight wagged his head and smacked his lips. "Ah," he went, while looking at his empty plate sort of sadly. Mr. Burberry ordered him two more korndogs.

"Mr. Blight, do you think our countrymen would find korndogs a tasty dish, were they to become available at home?"

"Oh, indeed, sir, indeed. A very pecooliarly fine flavor, these korndogs, especially with this special sauce you recommend."

"I am considering the possibility of becoming a korndog exporter, Mr. Blight."

"Well, sir, I believe you might make a good bit of cash from such an adventure."

"Yes. Yes." Mr. Burberry looked like he was thinking. He kept smiling. Mr. Burberry hauled out his wad of bills and paid up, after which he took Mr. Blight by the arm and the two of them marched off around the corner and down Fourth Street under Mr. Burberry's umbrella, happy in the rain as clams in cold water.

Cod shuffled back to his office. I spent the rest of the day thinking about how to get rich. Maybe I could get into Mr. Burberry's exporting business with both feet.

# 21
## Simon Burberry

It was good to chat with a countryman after all these weeks of deprivation, although Blight and I had little in common socially. His accent and demeanor were charming at first, in their slovenly way reminding me of home. They did quickly grow tiresome, especially as he continued to peer at me as if he could not believe I was not Silas Blade in disguise.

It was after midnight when Blade finally appeared from Mrs. Splinters's bathroom. Blight was much relieved to see him.

"It's been worth the trip after all, Mr. Blade, sir! I truly could not believe the other gentleman." Blight was ready to reveal the true reason for his search efforts and his presence in Balona.

"I'm sure you will want to know why I've come, Mr. Blade, sir!" He was courteous, respectful, unthreatening, ready to discuss details. "We maybe need to make some negotiations."

But as usual Blade was impatient. His eager desire to show off the inner workings of King Korndog quickly took precedence, and we were at the plant in short order. Blight was duly impressed, frequently expressing his surprise and admiration at the size and scope of the operation.

"I would truly like to see the entire process in action, sir, and when they are finally baking the product."

I pointed out how that part of the process began at about 4:00AM when the bakers arrive for duty. I observed that the present time was but 2:00AM and that we needed therefore to return to the now unattended chopper hopper so that I could make some adjustments.

"Ah, sir, have you become qualified so soon?"

"Oh, yes. I am what is known as a *quick study*." Under the circumstances, I felt it was unnecessary to discuss with him my talents in *vajramukti*, an art whose essential elements one may learn by correspondence.

So at last Blight has gone home, having had the experience of a lifetime and having left me his cap as another souvenir of his visit.

Mother Crinkle gives me worried glances if I am absent until late at night. She is difficult to mollify if I arrive home in the early hours of the morning. But there are times when one requires privacy. I must get back to the garage and work on my boxes.

But before I proceed with satisfying such needs, I must begin—as Mr. D. H. Carp has suggested—"pressing the flesh." This remarkably appropriate expression may be defined as the simple acts of shaking hands and kissing Balona babies. In fact, there appear to be few babes in arms visible on Balona streets, but there is no shortage of adult hands to be clasped. I began that very noon at the vegetable display in Mr. D. H. Carp's Groceries & Sundries. The first hand extended for my grip was that of a Mr. Donald Keyshot, a boffinish chap who lives above the store.

"How's things, Mr. Burberry?"

"I am in splendid health, Mr. Keyshot, mentally as well as physically." Mr. Keyshot, a gaunt fellow, tall as I, grasped my hand briefly but powerfully. "Perhaps I can count on your vote, Mr. Keyshot." I showed my teeth.

"As a friendly offering to a newcomer, Mr. Burberry, I must let you know at once that when a Balonan asks you *how's things*, he or she is only mouthing an idiomatic expression. Balonans do not expect a specific response, only another *how's things.* "

"Ah. How interesting." I thanked Mr. Keyshot for the information.

"I've got my office upstairs, too, Mr. Burberry, so if you ever need any advising, well, I'm up there. It's not a large place, but it's comfortable." Mr. Keyshot is said to be a professional "counselor," one who provides therapy and consolation for the emotionally afflicted, the rejected, the worried, and perhaps, the bored. I had heard about Mr. Keyshot's skills from Mrs. Shaw who was voluble on the subject.

"As to the voting, Mr. Burberry, I haven't yet cast a vote in any municipal election. Perhaps I will this time. I was reading an interesting item recently and discovered that in 1992 the Finnish Green Party garnered almost 150,000 votes. I'm not completely *green* myself. Nor Finnish actually." Mr. Keyshot chuckled. I noted that Mr. Keyshot did not commit himself to a position, my way or the other.

"I suppose you are acquainted with my opponent."

"I know who Mrs. Kuhl is, yes. She's the mother of young Joseph Kuhl whom I now know quite well. Joseph continues to grow taller, I notice."

"I intend to be quite flexible, Mr. Keyshot."

"I see. Well, I'm told that flexibility is a necessary quality in any Balona official. There was an interesting article recently on cognitive flexibility and constructivism....Well.... Yes." Mr. Keyshot selected vegetables, then went on to bread, tinned fish, and dry dogfood—small amounts of everything except the dogfood.

"I am naturally reserved, Mr. Keyshot, but I am told that in Balona a candidate must be somewhat forward, even personal, in launching a political campaign. So I shall remark that it appears from your choice of groceries that you may have a dog."

"Yes, Lamont and I are a pair." Mr. Keyshot selected dry macaroni in a plastic bag.

"And you sometimes advise persons generally, although those persons may have no mental or emotional complaint." This remark popped out without my thinking what I was suggesting, thus possibly creating the wrong impression—the mistaken impression that I might be seeking counseling.

"Ah." Mr. Keyshot ceased his shopping behavior, turned to look at me. "Yes. Yes, I do advise generally, as you put it. Yes, you put it nicely. Yes." His eyebrows rose. He smiled, perhaps sensing a potential client. Mr. Keyshot has a tannish complexion, brown eyes, not as dark as my beaver-browns, and a full head of brown hair turning white. He may be in his fifties. Older than I, but perhaps more fit.

"Mr. D. H. Carp is my political advisor, y'know, Mr. Keyshot."

"I didn't know that. No, I didn't. But I've been told that Mr. Carp is an excellent political advisor."

We stood in the aisle near the baked goods, he looking at the bread display, I examining the HoHos.

"But I have no other kind of advisor."

"Ah. I see. You don't. Well, in my own life I have found that it has been advisable at times to have a sort of advisor-in-general, a person I could turn to in troubled times."

Mr. Keyshot surely was trolling for clients. "Oh, I have no troubles, Mr. Keyshot. No troubled times. In fact I have never been happier, never felt lighter-spirited, y'know. No troubles at all. No." It was true that as of this morning, after two of the new capsules, my trembling had all but ceased.

"You are a very fortunate man, Mr. Burberry. I have felt that way occasionally—happy, light-spirited. But we are all damaged, y'know. Life will do that to our spirits, just as those free-radicals will damage our cells, as you may well know." He showed his teeth and looked past me toward the tinned vegetables. "Fortunately, there are always anti-oxidants. And hope."

Hope. The remark was touching. Were I the sentimental type, it might have brought tears to my eyes. But I felt Blade's presence and recovered quickly.

"Aha! Here you are, you two most stylish gentlemen of Balona!" Mrs. Shaw's voice was higher and louder than really necessary. Her lips were painted a very disturbing red. She looked up at us, swiveling her glance from one to the other. "You almost resemble each other. Do you know that?"

Not true. But women often have odd perceptions, or perhaps she was preparing some kind of argument. Lady Demelza enjoyed employing that technique. Mrs. Shaw peered into Mr. Keyshot's basket. "You are going to waste away, Don, eating like this. You need some meat and potatoes. Shall I fix you some?"

"I have macaroni and tuna here, Bell. Sufficient unto the need. The tuna, as you may well know, is said nowadays to be dolphin-free."

"Well, now. Why don't you invite Mr. Burberry and me up to your place for tea?" Mrs. Shaw made a show of examining her wristwatch. "It's that time, it'n it, Mr. Burberry? Tea time?"

"Any time is a good time for tea with friends, Mrs. Shaw."

Mrs. Shaw face and neck turned pink, then pinker. "My, how gallant! It'n he gallant, Don!"

"Won't you join me for tea?" Mr. Keyshot smiled, I thought rather weakly. Mrs. Shaw and I watched while Mr. Sackworth, Miss Patella's father, totted up Mr. Keyshot's purchases. Mr. D. H. Carp stood by, nodding and rubbing his hands. It would appear that Mr. Carp approved of my political associations.

Mr. Keyshot at once snapped on a radio which was playing classical music of some tinkling kind at low volume. "Corelli," he remarked. I am not musical, except for my whistling ability, and did not recognize the tune. Mr. Keyshot's quarters are spartan. Scandinavian furniture. Clean window glass. No unwashed cups in the sink. A black dog rose from a shallow box situated next to an overstuffed chair, looked hard at me, returned to its box without the usual sniffing and snuffling that dogs will perform on a stranger. "I do believe your dog likes me."

"That may be, Mr. Burberry. Lamont exercises considerable discretion in his friendships. If he likes you, he'll let you know. If he doesn't, he won't. A civilised dog."

I found the description of a dog as *civilised* amusing, and I chuckled. "Young Zachary Burnross's little dog has possibly similar discretion."

"Oh, it'n little Zachary a darling!"

"Little Zachary returned my case to the *Courier* office when he found it, y'know. I would have been bereft without it. Little Zachary is an honest youth."

Mrs. Shaw was leafing through magazines, peering into Mr. Keyshot's bookcases, lifting papers, rearranging things. Mr. Keyshot commanded us, civilly, "Do take a seat, both of you. Yes, there are a few honest youths still around. Perhaps a dying breed." Mr. Keyshot was bustling about with tea things.

"Honesty is still the best policy, is it not, Mr. Keyshot!"

"Elphinstone, as you may well know, mentioned that it is an objective of good teachers to try to instill honesty in their students, if their parents are unable and the media unwilling. Of course, Elphinstone would not have used the phrase 'the media,' *per se*."

"I have always admired teachers." I have *never* admired teachers, believing them to be generally an ignorant and servile lot, but a politic lie was appropriate.

"I admire Don. He is so discreet. And he is such a fine counselor. He knows about everything. And he usually knows just what you're thinking."

"My, I hope not!"

"Bell's of course exaggerating, as you may well know, Mr. Burberry. I simply try to apply my training in the light of my experience."

"Don was a soldier as well as a teacher and a counselor."

"Bell, I was not a soldier."

"You said..."

"I was a United States Marine." Unconsciously, Mr. Keyshot drew himself to attention over his tea things.

"Well, same thing. Were you a soldier, Mr. Burberry?"

"I am unable to respond to the question, Mrs. Shaw. Secrets, y'know."

Mr. Keyshot and Mrs. Shaw both turned and looked closely at me. "Change the subject, Bell." Mr. Keyshot began pouring.

"Well, if you can't talk about your service, you must be in some kind of special occupation, right?"

"Do you suppose it will continue raining through election day, Mrs. Shaw?"

"Mr. Burberry's the one who's changing the subject, Don! It'n that exciting! I'll have to put that in my column."

"You are planning to include me in your column, Mrs. Shaw?"

"I wish you'd call me Bellona. I finally got Don to call me Bell, but he knows me better than you, so you call me Bellona, okay?"

"I would be delighted to call you Bellona, Bellona." I laughed, not loudly.

Mrs. Shaw quivered. Mr. Keyshot's dog raised its head and growled.

"Lamont! What's got into you? Lamont never growls. Settle down, Lamont."

The dog continued its raised-head gaze, fixed on me. I bluffed it out, as American card-players say. "What have I done, Lamont?" The animal did not respond, except to shake its head, turn to Mr. Keyshot, and emit a groan. "Perhaps it wants out?"

"Lamont and I make our recreational circuit twice a day. It's too early for Lamont's needs. Besides, if it's an emergency, Lamont has a special box behind the door there. It's often said that only cats will use a box like that, but Lamont is the exception that proves the rule. Lamont is not only civilised, he's considerate."

"Perhaps it's hungry." The beast lay down and covered its head with its paws.

"Lamont sometimes expresses dissatisfaction with tastes and odors and sounds. He's a discriminating dog."

"Yes. Well, a dog is a dog in my experience." An impolitic remark. I recovered at once. "Of course, this animal is obviously an exception, a rare creature."

I finished my tea and made my exit as soon as it appeared decent to do so, leaving Mrs. Shaw to finish her tea with Mr. Keyshot and the dog. The dog's behavior was quite upsetting. Perhaps it saw something the others did not perceive. Some animals are said to be prescient.

The trembling has begun again. Nevertheless, I shall bash on.

# 22

## Joseph Oliver Kuhl

When I have a problem, I used to go to my Cousin Nimitz MacArthur Chaud, sit down there in his comfy leather "victim's chair" and unload. Cousin Nim is Pastor of Balona's BoMFog Tabernacle and a hero and a huge guy with two doctor's degrees. Everybody loves him, or at least likes him.

Problem with going to Cousin Nim is, he always expects you to *do* something about your problem. What I like to do is *think* about my problem, worry about it a little, feel sort of sorry for myself about it, and then maybe take quite a while to do anything about it. It's the thinking-about-it part that can be the pleasurable part of having a problem.

So lately I've been going on up to see Mr. Keyshot when I've got something on my mind that I don't want to let Zack in on. It is a fact that Zack is smarter than me. He thinks stuff a lot faster. He's got more ideas. I actually feel like a dumb clod around that little high school kid.

Mr. Keyshot is a lot smarter than me, too. But Mr. Keyshot doesn't smirk and nod his head when I admit I don't know something, the way Zack does. Sometimes Zack even sets me up. What I mean is, Zack will twist the conversation around to where I'm talking about something *he* wants to talk about. Then he'll ask me a question that I don't know the answer to. Then he will answer his own question. Then he will wag his head and make a big sigh, like Joseph Oliver Kuhl is just the dumbest dunce in Balona. I have a name for it. I call it "Zack's trope."

So that's why I sometimes don't tell stuff to Zack or Cousin Nim, and instead go on up to Mr. Keyshot's place. There's one more reason, of course. Mr. Keyshot sort of respects me being a practicer of tradecraft. What I mean to say is, it's sort of tit for tat, as we say in Balona. Since I don't have any cash to pay him for listening, I give him tradecraft tips from my studies of Criminal Justice and my knowledge of the UITS Manual.

One of the things I have been losing valuable sleep about lately is the campaign of Bapsie Kuhl for office. My ma is the kind of a person who is a huge pain to all the people around her, especially the people in her family. What she has done now, is take her 20-year-old high school Korndog Kween picture—with she wearing her Krown (before it got sat on and squashed, of course)—and had Mr. Preene print up posters showing "Vote for Kween Bapsie." Did I say 20? Actually 20-plus. She has put up these posters with that picture on it all over Balona. She's got four in the front windows of Mr. D. H. Carp's Groceries & Sundries. I feel like wearing my terrorist cap pulled down all the way so people don't recognize me as a relation of "Kween Bapsie." What a pain!

If she's a pain being just a wife and ma and candidate, you can imagine what kind of pain she would be if she actually got to be Mayor of Balona.

First of all, she says, she would get herself a private secretary. A big handsome man with a mustache, she says, to follow her around town and take notes on her thoughts. She plans to publish her thoughts every Saturday in the *Courier*. Mr. Preene has already agreed. These thoughts will be about how she intends to make Balona a more satisfying place for her to live in.

For example, the first thought she said the other day was, "All the *dum-shik* cats in town ought to be strangled. They poop on your garden and they make noises all night. Who needs 'em."

Dad right away went, "You cut'n say that, Baps, honey. There's lots of cat lovers in town. They'd never stand for it."

"They'd have to stand for it, since I'd be Mayor, and what I say goes!" Ma got sort of a wild look in her green eye. (The other one is blue, but the green one is the one that usually gets the wild look.)

"Well, you better not say it out loud, or you'd never get elected in the first place."

After saying that, Dad had to sleep at the office. At least he had a nice raincoat to wear on the way.

"Where'd that raincoat come from?" went Dad later. "It's too big around and too long for me, but it sure keeps you dry. And it smells good, too."

I changed the subject since I didn't want to admit I found it in a Runcibles in the Mall shopping bag at the dump along with the galoshes and Ma's gift muumuu, et cetera.

Anyway, this business of Ma's campaign is one of the problems I started to talk about with Mr. Keyshot, up at his place.

The rain was coming down and making a roar on the roof. Mr. Keyshot had some nice piano music playing on his CD machine which he turned up a little so we could hear it. He had made us some tea, which I don't like but was drinking to be polite.

"It seems to me," he went, "if your mom made some speeches about her beliefs and intentions, then the voters would get an idea of whether they want her as mayor—or not." He slurped on his tea and raised up his eyebrows, a trope that calls for a response from your conversational victim.

"You mean I should tell her she needs to make some speeches?"

"As you may well know, Joseph, Balona voters nowadays are a bit more sophisticated than they were only a few years ago. In fact, the voters may even be a bit *jaded*."

I didn't recall the vocabulary word, but it sounded suave, so I got out my notebook and wrote *jaded* in there, for possible use in some emergency. "Well," I went, "Balona voters haven't bothered to vote in a real long time, I heard, so who knows what they think?"

"Precisely." We sat there drinking our tea, him looking into his cup, nodding his head in time to the music and the rain, kind of like the way Cousin Nim does. Me, looking at Lamont. Lamont sleeping, as usual.

I told him about the Kween posters, and about how Ma threw Dad out of the house when he suggested she shouldn't tell everybody about her political platform, since if she did, nobody would elect her.

"Yes, I noticed the posters. As you may well know, they are noticeable." Mr. Keyshot sort of smiled into his cup and didn't ask anything about my Ma's political platform. He is sure a confidential guy. I noticed Mr. Keyshot's copy of the *Courier* on the lamp table next to his chair.

"Mrs. Shaw sort of slaughtered my ma, what with her column, wut'n you say?"

"Mrs. Shaw will say she was being even-handed, which is what she says she usually tries to be in her writings, as you may well know."

"If my ma ever gets around to reading that column, she'll grab Mrs. Shaw by the hair and throw her down our front steps."

"I should probably mention that possibility to Mrs. Shaw next time I see her."

I reached over and got the paper off of his table, opened it up, folded it to where Mrs. Shaw's column took a whole skinny side of the page.

Bellona Covers Balona
by Bellona Shaw

Anybody who has ever played bridge with Barbara Balona "Bapsie" Chaud-Kuhl knows that she is a fierce competitor, even barefooted. Mr. Simon Burberry, on the other hand, is a true English gentleman, who is tall, handsome, soft-spoken, and well shod at all times.

It is well known that Mrs. Chaud-Kuhl talks a great deal about her flexibility. Mr. Burberry, an artistic craftsman who builds beautiful puzzle boxes in his spare time, is reputed to be a person of considerable flexibility.

Mrs. Chaud-Kuhl has several times challenged Mr. Burberry to arm wrestling matches. Mr. Burberry has not responded, but has mentioned to this columnist that he would be delighted to engage in a debate "on the issues."

"What issues?" said Mrs. Chaud-Kuhl. "I'll tell you what the issues are after I have been elected."

In an exciting and creative surprise move by Mr. Sam Joe Sly, that korndog magnate offered Mr. Burberry an executive position with King Korndog Inkorporated, and Mr. Burberry has accepted. The firm has just announced that it proposes to begin negotiations to export King Korndogs to the United Kingdom. "This is one flexible guy," reports Mr. Sly of Mr. Burberry. Flexibility is said to be a chief characteristic desired in a Balona mayor.

Mrs. Chaud-Kuhl has said she has several important matters to take care of as soon as she is elected. What those matters are, she did not choose to elaborate on to this columnist. "You'll find out soon enough. But I'll give you a hint. Your garden won't be messed up, and you'll get more sleep when I'm elected."

Balonans appear to have a clear choice in the upcoming mayoral election.

"Mrs. Shaw is sort of leaning towards Mr. Burberry, wut'n you say?"

"Rutherford B. Hays and Samuel Tilden had a close race in 1876, as you may well know. And the 1960 Presidential race was very close, not to speak of the Florida affair more recently."

"You mean my ma might win? It's that close, you think?"

"Well, possibly, or perhaps not, Joseph. I was simply searching for comparisons. But, as you may well know, your mother does have supporters, as has Mr. Burberry."

"How do you figure you'll vote?"

"Well, now, that's a question better unanswered for, as you may well know, I am acquainted with both of the candidates and would like to remain neutral in regard to my political leanings." Mr. Keyshot frowned into his cup. "*Remain neutral* was an inappropriate phrase. I must stop thinking of myself as neutral. What I mean to say is, I do have an opinion. Would you like another cup?"

Mr. Keyshot is acquainted with tradecraft because of me telling him about a bunch of techniques, so he just changed the subject on me. I guess he doesn't want to tell me who he's going to vote for.

We sat there and listened to the music and the rain for a while. Then I made my excuses (schoolwork, philosophical thoughts, et cetera), and went over to Zack's. He was up in his bedroom gluing up a couple of boards and sticks to make a little stage, so that Harley can see out of the window seat window without having to raise up his head.

"You're sure good to that animal."

"Harley is a sensitive creature who requires cosseting." (Zack's vocabulary again.) Harley was laying there on the window seat. He didn't open up his eyes, but he raised one eyebrow, like Mr. Burberry does, as if to say, "See, I told you."

I mentioned that I had been talking to Mr. Keyshot about the mayor campaign.

Zack changed the subject, mentioning right away that he had been studying Mr. Burberry's private papers, copies of which Zack has got a whole boxfull of. He was pressing his two boards together to make the glue stick, so he pointed at his desk with his chin. "Take a look at that and give me your opinion on what it means. The paper right in the middle there."

It was Zack's copy of a page from one of Mr. Burberry's (or Mr. Blade's) notebooks.

> *To honor one's friends, one must eat them with pride. To savor the deliciousness of his meat, to understand his being through our most essential, pure act: eating. There is no better way to honor someone; we are what we eat.*

"Well, if it's not just poetry, it's probably Mr. Burberry had a sort of cow friend or maybe a sheep he was fond of."

"I don't think Mr. Burberry is a waiter any more," went Zack. "I think maybe he's already sitting down at the table, a special kind of a guy—a gourmet."

# 23
### Simon Burberry

As I have committed myself to campaigning for office, and winning, I have made the decision to go about it systematically. I need allies and supporters who are respectworthy. Mr. D. H. Carp is an ally, but I suspect he may not be held in great respect by the majority of the populace. His grocery prices are exorbitant.

Residents speak of Pastor Nim Chaud with respect, even with awe, but I have not met Pastor Chaud. He is a cousin of Mrs. Chaud-Kuhl, as his surname might suggest, and that very fact might disqualify him from supporting my candidacy. A great many Balonans seem to be cousins. In that characteristic, Balonans are much like denizens of my own home village.

Mr. Kenworth Burnross is a pleasant fellow when he is focused. His law practice is not thriving. Those facts offer one benefits of sorts, but not political benefits.

Mr. Patrick Preene and Mrs. Bellona Shaw repute themselves as "balanced," and that puts them out of the running as political advisors. Besides, Mrs. Shaw is intrusive and, one might say, bossy.

Mr. Kenworth Kuhl and son Joseph are out of the question.

Of the Balona residents I have now met in person, Mr. Keyshot appears to be one who is well respected. He once mentioned that he considers everyone to be "damaged," and is thus likely to be sympathetic to one with odd characteristics. Therefore, I decided to make it known to Mother Crinkle that I am "seeking professional help" from Mr. Keyshot in order to "Americanize" me for office. Perhaps "Balonize" me would be more accurate. Mother Crinkle will surely circulate my intentions rapidly. I cannot imagine a speedier, more efficient channel.

Mr. Keyshot greeted me warmly and offered me tea which I accepted. The black dog eyed me but did not greet me. Tinkling music was in the background and, after we had settled down to our tea, I mentioned that the music was pleasant but that it tended to interfere with my thought processes. It is a fact that I am bound either to think or to hear music or to speak. I cannot perform all of those operations at once.

"That is indeed interesting, Mr. Burberry." Mr. Keyshot turned the music off and we listened to the rain for a moment. It has continued to rain for several days, seemingly day and night.

"I am sorry about that, sir. I know you like music."

"Not a problem. Albert Einstein, as you may well know, could listen only to instrumental music while at work. It was his observation that vocal music required one to listen to the words, to comprehend, to respond intellectually. I found that quite interesting, as it is also true of me. But serious music of any kind seems to pullulate ideas in me!"

I pulled out my notebook and pen, wrote *pullulate*, hoped I had it spelled correctly, but was not about to ask.

"Are you mathematical?"

His first question. Direct but discreet. Mr. Keyshot is more subtle than I thought. A good sign. Or perhaps not a good sign.

"I have been diagnosed professionally as obsessive-compulsive, sir. And I have occasions of terrible dreams and inexpressible thoughts. And I am a somnambulist of sorts. And I do love my mother. But I am neither mathematician nor musician. And I am not here to discuss those other personal grievances, sir. I am here for political advice."

"Oh."

"I chose you as a possible advisor because I have heard from a variety of sources that you are a sensible person." Of course, I did not mention Mother Crinkle's jaundiced assessment.

Mr. Keyshot sipped and turned pink. "First time in a long time that I've been accused of being a sensible person!" He chuckled. We chuckled. "Alex Ordway has much wisdom. Kosh Chaud has considerable political savvy. Political sense I have little."

"I do not know those men, and I do know something of you. And I have hope that you may be of assistance. And of course I am a paying customer."

"First off, let me say that we refer to our customers as *clients*, Mr. Burberry. The term takes the rough commercial edge off our transactions. With a physician, the customer is known as a *patient*, as you may well know. That term predisposes the customer to wait patiently and uncomplainingly. Clever don't you think?"

135

"I had never thought about it, but now that you mention it, yes."

"We Balonans are going to celebrate our Sugarbeet Festival soon, as you may well know." Mr. Keyshot seems to have a habit of going off-track in his conversations.

"I did not know. I'm assuming that the sugarbeet is a Balona product?"

"The sugarbeet was once Balona's pre-eminent product. That was before the world sugar glut, the massive introduction of sugar substitutes, and the rise of King Korndog and the turkey factory."

"Very interesting, I'm sure." I put my cup on the low table. "Has this something to do with politics, sir?"

"You needn't call me *sir*, Mr. Burberry. I barely made it to lance corporal." Mr. Keyshot twinkled.

"Just a habit of speech, is all. Of course, I myself am a commander. In mufti now, of course, and in secret." Those items slipped out. My hand inadvertently covered my mouth.

"Hm? Ah, yes. I see. Yes. Well, you ask if the Sugarbeet Festival has anything to do with politics. And I respond, saying that in my opinion the Sugarbeet Festival is *all* about politics. In the first place, it's held in the spring because it's politically convenient. The actual sugarbeet harvest takes place in the fall. In the second place, the festival is the occasion at which politicians make their most impressive pitches, spend most of their money, put out their posters. Of course, the festival also features crafts and contests and demonstrations and dancing and foods,"

"I see. I enjoy different kinds of foods." Again I spoke without thinking.

"Foods. Oh, yes. The Sugarbeet Festival is the occasion at which Balona cooks strut their stuff. Lots of different foods are offered then. Yes."

"I do like korndogs."

"Yes. Well, to each his own. I enjoy spinach *quiche*." He twinkled again, and was obviously trading confidence for confidence, but I was lost in my own reminiscences.

"We have a dish we call Star Gazy Pie."

"Sounds, uh, heavenly."

"I enjoy it very much. You take these little fish—pilchards, y'know—and you wrap them up in dough but you leave the little heads protruding, outside the wrap, y'know. And then you bake them and the little fish are right there, well baked, but peeping out at the stars, y'know. That's why we call it Star Gazy Pie, y'know. Yes, I miss that dish."

"I haven't heard of that dish, Mr. Burberry."

"I enjoy fish. But I especially enjoy meat."

"Indeed. Well."

"Especially rare meats."

"Ah. Rare meats, I see. If I ever eat meat, I prefer mine well done."

"That wasn't quite the definition of *rare* I was referring to. But let that pass. You believe I should prepare a speech for Sugarbeet Festival, do you? "

"I believe it would be prudent to do so. Yes." Mr. Keyshot looked at me keenly. Perhaps I had been indiscreet.

"About my *commander* remark? I sometimes exaggerate, y'know, for dramatic effect. A habit I picked up in my travels."

"I see."

"Yes. So, you believe I should speak out. When is the Sugarbeet Festival to take place?

"It is scheduled when the Town Council decrees. No one seems to know at the moment. But I suspect they will announce the dates soon, as the festival always occurs before an election. Of course, there haven't been any elections in recent years."

"How have officials been elected?"

"Hm. I suppose they haven't exactly been elected. Rather, they have been *selected*. However, I supposed the Town Fathers were looking for a little fun, so they decided to have an actual election. Unusual. Ah, but for a truly unusual election, take the Nova Scotia election of 1999. Now there was an unusual...." I was now giving quite a keen and puzzled look at Mr. Keyshot, and he trailed off. "...but that's not really germane to our discussion here, I suppose. Mm, all of us have peculiarities, I suppose."

"I myself, sir, have a variety of peculiarities."

"Perhaps you could speak of them during your Sugarbeet Festival address."

"I think not. They are likely far *too* peculiar, even for Balona."

"Well, Mr. Burberry, so far you have mentioned your compulsive nature, and your tendency to exaggerate at times, and some of your dietary enjoyments. Is there something specific we could discuss? Something you wanted to get off your chest, as we say in Balona?"

Mr. Keyshot had listened carefully, more carefully than his offhand manner would indicate. I determined to be cautious in what I divulged. "Some agents are...were after me, y'know. It's not something I want to get off my chest, as you say, but rather a matter I do not myself clearly understand. I can think of nothing important for which I should be sought by international agents."

"You can think of nothing important."

"Yes, nothing."

"I see. You have an interesting hobby, I hear."

"Ah. The boxes. Yes, I do those well, I must say."

"You have been doing those for a long time?"

"I don't really remember when I began. It was someone else began, y'know, and I simply caught on."

"Pardon?"

"I am troubled by very red hair worn by mid-age to elderly women, y'know."

"I would say many people may be troubled by that phenomenon."

"No, sir. I mean *troubled*." It was out. I debated in the moment if I should continue. "I did mention the compulsions. Did I mention the capsules? No? The capsules help to control the trembling. But the red hair often overcomes the beneficial effects of the capsules. Do you know, I had to seek an herbalist to concoct my capsules in Delta City. They seem to calm my spirit. And the boxes. Yes, the boxes help, too. Manufacturing them as I do helps focus my attention."

"Well, there you are!" Mr. Keyshot clapped his hands, surprising and awakening the black dog. "Sorry, Lamont. But there's your text for the Sugarbeet Festival."

"Pardon?"

"You can speak about how in our tension-filled world, one needs releases. Your boxes, Mr. Burberry, your boxes help you not only to focus but, as you may well know, they help you release your pent-up tensions. Yes, I would say you have a winner there. Mrs. Shaw writes columns. Mr. D. H. Carp focuses his attention on how he might eventually win a Congressional seat. Young Zachary Burnross explores the Balona Dump. I myself listen to fine music that helps me think while I ponder how to assist my clients. We all must find our own way to a constructive resolution of our tensions. You could build a splendid little speech on how you have been helped—and rendered ever more flexible—by constructing your boxes."

"Yes, I could speak on that subject. Easily."

"And you could offer one of your boxes as a prize at the Sugarbeet Festival, could you not?" His expression clouded. "Of course, just one of those boxes must take an enormous amount of your time and energy to fabricate, and must therefore be of considerable value to you. Perhaps I spoke out of turn."

"No. You are absolutely on target, Mr. Keyshot. I could, in fact, offer a number of my boxes as prizes, for transporting them about has become a chore. Thank you. You have made my day!"

We proceeded in that vein for a time, and as I left, both of us were in fine spirits.

# 24
## Joseph Oliver Kuhl

"They're sure heavy, Mr. Burberry! How come they're so heavy? There's something inside here, it'n there?" Me and Zack were hauling Mr. Burberry's boxes from his closet out to his car. We were getting a fee for helping him, he said, but he didn't say how much. He is going to display his boxes in Mr. D. H. Carp's front windows. Showing them off, since they are going to be prizes in one of the Sugarbeet Festival drawings.

"Well, let me see." He picked up a box, hefted it, looked at the ceiling. "No. it's not inordinately heavy. You see, mm, I make my boxes from extra-heavy wood, mm, so that they won't tip over."

"Well, of course. They're cubes. Cubes're not likely to tip over." Zack sort of shook the box he was carrying.

"Oh, no, Zachary. You don't want to do that. It might, mm, disturb the puzzle mechanism, y'see."

"Oh. Okay." Zack was mumbling again, and letting me do most of the heavy lifting. Zack usually wears his neckbrace. Mr. Burberry commented on it.

"Well, Zachary. I do hope the weight of one of my boxes doesn't result in a whiplash injury." He crinkled his eyes and chuckled in his nose.

"Don't worry about that. I'm waiting for deeper pockets." Then Zack stood up straight, frowned his face in thought, and said, "Hmm," as if he was thinking again about the contents of Mr. Burberry's briefcase and re-considering Mr. Burberry as a possible deep-pockets candidate.

"Ha ha ha," went Mr. Burberry. "You have a splendid sense of humor, Zachary." Zack liked that and stopped frowning right away. Zack always likes to be complimented. I have learned in my travels along life's path, in fact, that most guys like to be complimented. Guys that really don't deserve the compliment enjoy it most and smirk about it longest. My ma would never compliment a guy. I can see that Mr. Burberry has got a definite advantage in the compliment department.

"I was wondering, Mr. Burberry." Zack always has got to try an angle while I am lifting and carrying and arranging boxes.

"Yes, Zachary. You were wondering."

"I was thinking that when you get to be mayor you will need a public relations agent. You know, somebody to go around telling people how suave you are, how many good things you're doing. That sort of thing. I suppose you've got a publicity agent in mind already."

"Frankly, Zachary, I hadn't given that position much thought." He looked at me and Zack both. "Are you chaps both interested in such a position?"

"I'm the one interested," went Zack, not even giving me a chance to answer back. "Joe's got all he can manage with his classes coming up in the second semester over at C4. He's got to pass this time, or he's out in the cold again." Zack was being sort of kind, giving me an out. I didn't know whether to be grateful or PO'd (polite C4 expression for the rude Balona way of saying it: *pissed off*), since he was also dissing me. I still haven't figured out a way to take him down a peg or two.

"Publicity. Well, I'll certainly consider the possibility." Mr. Burberry looked over each of his boxes as we had stacked them in his trunk and on the seats of his car.

"I see you've got a Ford here, Mr. Burberry." Zack had his fingers all over the place where the Ford gizmo had been pried off the car.

"I believe it's an Aston-Martin, Zachary."

"Oh, no, Mr. Burberry. You got screwed, I'm afraid, if you thought you bought an Aston-Martin. You got a Ford here."

"Ah. Well. One does live and learn. Yes." Mr. Burberry's face got sort of dark and he polished a box with his hanky pretty hard. He gave Zack a hard look. "How do you know it's not an Aston-Martin, Zachary?"

"Well, you just look at the Ford ads, and you remember the pictures, and you take a look at the Aston-Martin ads and you remember those pictures, and you've got it figured. That's how. And you can figure out that this is a rental, too, not a purchase."

"And how might one determine that as a fact?"

"Well, you just look at the little tag pasted on back here, Mr. Burberry. That tells you." Zack stretched his neck and looked at the inside of the front door on the driver's side. "You got some work to do on that door there, Mr. Burberry. Right there where the little white things are trying to hold the door panel on. Looks like somebody took the panel off and cut'n get it back on again."

"Yes, it was I who did that. Attempting to make some, mm, adjustments myself. Afraid I'm a fine craftsman with wood but not so fine with mechanical things."

"Oh, I am. I'm fine with mechanical things—and wood, too. Also metal and plastic. Dit'n I mention that before?" Zack smirked at me. "I could fix that door for you, no sweat."

"My word! Could you indeed? I would be willing to compensate you for your work."

"Yeh, of course." Zack's eyes got all beady. He cast his vision sideways at me. "It would be another twenty is all."

"You said *another* twenty. Whence came the first twenty?"

"Oh, we just finished it, me and Joe here. We just finished our $20 worth of labors. Mr. Burberry, in Balona you always got to agree on the price *before* you start on the job."

"I see. I regret to inform you young chaps that it is against my principles to pay more than the going minimum wage for plain hard labor."

"Aha! But we have done *special soft* labor, not *plain hard* labor. Special soft labor requires that we took care and dit'n drop anything. Or shake up anything. And we placed it in a very special way, eksedra. Not plain hard labor at all." Zack now gave Mr. Burberry a hard look. "We thought we were dealing with a flexible guy, Mr. Burberry. Besides," Zack grabbed at his neckbrace, "I think a may have twisted my neck just now, while doing work on your project here." Zack started to limp a little, too. "I hope you got workman's compensation."

"You mentioned you intended to become a jurist?"

"Oh, before that I'm gonna be a lawyer, of course."

"Mm-hm. I can see that." Mr. Burberry turned to me. "Well, Joseph. What do you think of all this?"

"Hey, me and Zack are blood related. I bet he could bring his toolbox over here after lunch and fix that door for you in a few minutes. And you'd have a nice fixed door instead of a beat up ruined-looking door in there. A door you could be proud of." I smirked at Zack, and he smirked back. It's not always a bad thing if your cousin happens to be a little quicker than you.

Mr. Burberry stood there scratching his chin, looking at the gutter. He scratched again. "I guess you have me," he went, and reached into his pocket for his wad of bills. "Are you going to help me unload these boxes at Mr. D. H. Carp's and arrange them in his windows, or is that to be another twenty?"

"Oh, no, Mr. Burberry. It's all part of this here job. We wut'n cheat you, y'know. We can wait for our pay until we finish the job."

Mr. Burberry smiled, stuffed the wad back into his pocket. A nice guy. Flexible. And rich. Which trope is even nicer.

After we helped arrange the boxes in Mr. D. H. Carp's windows, and put up with Mr. Carp and Mr. Stackworth telling Mr. Burberry how it should be done, and Mr. Burberry finally doing it exactly the way he wanted to, Mr. Burberry gave us our due. I went home for lunch and Zack went home to get his toolbox.

Ma had her bridge group there again. Mrs. Crinkle was going on about how Mr. Burberry was seeking professional help to make him a better Balonan.

Everybody commented on that while I was making my peanut butter sandwich. Then Mrs. Shaw made a bunch of remarks about how suave Mr. Burberry is and about how she was just about close to falling in love with him. Everybody commented about that while I was getting my can of Hires from the fridge.

And then they all commented about how maybe Mr. Keyshot would be better off without Mrs. Shaw. Mrs. Shaw then got mad and left the group and the game, slamming the front door. Then all the women laughed up a storm, my ma loudest.

"That Bellona Shaw is just a dumb foreigner," went Mrs. Crinkle.

"I thought you liked dumb foreigners," went my ma, making it plain that she was talking about Mr. Burberry, her rival.

"Oh, speaking of which, let me show you my postcards!" Mrs. Crinkle dragged out a stack of postcards and shuffled through the pack, muttering about each one. "No, that's from Henry. He's been dead and gone for 10 years now."

Apparently, Mrs. Crinkle keeps a lifetime supply of old postcards in her purse. Finally, she dragged two out of the pack. "Here's one from Bena. She says it's cold up there in Montana, but Card has a huge big house with three fireplaces and all kind of wood to burn, so she's warm as toast up there. See: 'Warm as toast over here,' she says here.

"And here's one from Mr. Burberry's ugly little friend Mr. Blight. Oh, it's the old Oliver. Dut'n that just wring out your heart to see that dear old building!" Mrs Crinkle is referring to the picture on the postcard of our old movie house which got burned down a couple years ago, but which Claire Preene, who owns it replaced it and calls the new building the New Oliver. "Mr. Blight's in Montana, too, maybe visiting Bena to let her know her house is okay. That sort of thing. Wat'n that nice of him? Nice for a foreigner to go all the way out of his way just to do that."

"Mr. Blight? I thought Mr. Blight was the one taking care of Bena's house so it wut'n get wrecked up by Arabs now that she's up there in Montana. He's left and gone already?" Aunt Sarah sounded really concerned. "I wonder who's taking care of Bena's place now that Mr. Blight has took off."

"Well, Sarah, I wut'n worry about it if I was you. Mr. Burberry don't leave nothing to chance. If he wants it took care of, it'll get took care of, never you mind." Mrs. Crinkle snatched her postcards back and re-examined them herself.

Then it was necessary to criticize Ma's posters. The critics were gentle. Aunt Pippa (Zack's ma) said she thought the posters "look striking."

Aunt Sarah said you could "see 'em from across the street they're that striking, especially the Krown part."

Mrs. Sasifrage wondered where Ma got the posters made.

Mrs. Trilbend said if she ever ran for office she might ask Ma for advice about posters.

Then it was quiet for a while, the ladies thinking thoughts, probably about how smart they were to avoid getting grabbed by the hair and thrown down our front steps.

"You decided yet to make a speech at Sugarbeet Festival when Mr. Burberry is gonna make his speech?"

"I haven't decided."

"You gonna give prizes, too, like Mr. Burberry's giving away his boxes as prizes."

"I haven't decided. I'm thinking about it."

Actually, Ma has already thought about it, and has decided to donate Dad's golf clubs, our old TV set, and a bunch of stuff down in the basement. Except for the golf clubs, Dad thought it was a good idea.

"Good idear, Baps, honey," he went about the giveaways, looking sort of sad and joyful at the same time.

Mrs. Sasifrage all at once pointed at Ma. "Say, Bapsie, you got you a new muumuu."

Everybody commented on the new muumuu.

"It's a present from my nice kid, Joey."

"Hey, that's nice to have a nice kid give you muumuus. Do you know, Bapsie, that muumuu looks just like Bena's muumuu."

Everybody stopped talking and drinking and eating. They were all looking at Ma's new muumuu.

"It sure does," went Mrs. Trilbend.

It couldn't be, since I had found the muumuu at the dump, and it is a well-known fact that before she went off to Montana, Mrs. Bena Splinters never threw anything away. It also occurred that I needed to get over to Mr. Burberry's place right away and watch Zack repair Mr. Burberry's car door panel, so I left by the back door, not bothering to retrieve my bomber jacket from the rack in the front hall.

# 25

## Simon Burberry

I have been faithful in taking my new capsules. Perhaps they are effective, but recently I have had about as much excitement as I am able to bear.

As an example to prove my point, I was having my breakfast coffee with Mother Crinkle. This is a ceremony we have come to enjoy, as she boils the hot water and spoons the formula into our cups. I pour the water. She adds the cream and sugar. We each stir, then touch cups across the table before we imbibe. It is exactly the ceremony that Mum and I used to participate in, but this was initiated by Mother Crinkle without any input from me at all. The dozy environment and the lovely coincidence of the act almost bring tears to my eyes each morning.

My darling Mum, I still recall, warned me about liaisons with women. Or men, either, for that matter. "Else you will be betrayed, child," she said, the mournful expression causing her face to sag, bloodhound-like under the red wig, especially the eye pouches and cheeks. I have heeded her words all my life, quickly backing away from possible entanglements, becoming therefore an ever more focused and loyal employee. It is strange, but Mother Crinkle is Mum-like—as long as she *eschews* her red wig. On the occasions of her wearing that dreadful thing, she has precipitated the trembling in me and the terrible thoughts. Well, I have given her fair warning.

We were having our coffee and toast, preparing to share the *Courier*, when the doorbell jangled. Mother Crinkle almost sprang to her feet and dashed to the door, or at least gave passable impressions of springing and dashing. "It's probably my seed catalog," she cried. But there continued to be considerable noise at the door, so I decided that Mother Crinkle might require my assistance. I picked up the marmalade knife and. quickly recalling instructions in the Manual, went to her rescue.

What should my eyes behold but Madog, standing there arguing with Mother Crinkle. "There's nobody by that name here," she was repeating, as if it were a mantra, "so you just get on your way and leave him alone." The bullying swine looked over Mother Crinkle's shoulder and spied me in my blue dressing gown and wearing my now-usual brown-and-black.

"Mr. Blade, sir!" he shouted. There was no trace of his usual flippancy.

I cannot imagine how he recognized me.

"Oh, sir! I've found you at last." To Mother Crinkle, he observed, "That there's Mr. Blade. It's the man himself I been looking for." Madog sounded reasonable, even courteous, even unctuous.

Mother Crinkle reached into the hall closet next to the front door. She held something at her side for a moment. "My! Look at that!" She was stretching her neck so as to look beyond Madog at something in the street.

The fellow naturally turned to see the object of her attention and, as he did, Mother Crinkle brought forth her baseball bat and fetched Madog a mighty blow to his crown. He fell heavily into the shrubbery at the side of the porch. The hit would have put the legendary batsman Joe Montana to shame.

"A sex fiend if I ever saw one, after a poor old woman, too." Mother Crinkle clucked several times, closed the door, and leaned her bat behind the door, perhaps in anticipation of an imminent revival.

"We should call the ambulance," I suggested.

"Sex fiends don't deserve such kind attention as you would give."

"Ah. But I trust you did not intend to slay him, so he is likely to revive, is he not? And then complain loudly and perhaps pursue legal action? This is, after all, a highly litigious society."

"I give him a smart one, Mr. Burberry, uh, Simon. He's not gonna revive right away."

"But perhaps, dear, it would be prudent to notify Constable Cod?"

"Yeh. Okay. You can do that. I'll make us some more nice cinnamon toast to go with our Postum." Mother Crinkle shuffled off to the kitchen, 98-years-old again, and I made my way to the phone.

An ambulance transported the unconscious and bleeding Madog to a hospital in Delta City where, I have been informed recently, other putative sex fiends have been taken after having made overtures on Mother Crinkle's porch.

The re-arrival of Madog does give opportunity to discover his business with me.  Blight had no opporunity to reveal his mission, so eager was Blade to show off the plant.  I am resolved to take some time—given Madog's recovery—to find out the wherefore of his appearance in Balona.

As Mr. Sam Joe Sly has ventured off to Reno, another city in the State of Nevada, a place where, it is said, one can win or lose a million dollars quickly, I am again in complete charge of King Korndog.  My success with the plant inspectors convinced Mr. Sly that his bringing me into the firm was a wise move.  However, Mr. Sly has not as yet offered a written contract nor any hard compensation for my services.  I am considering variations on plans of action.

Mrs. Kenworth Burnross, wife of my elderly solicitor, paid me a visit in the Crinkle living room recently.  "Well, I am the wife of your lawyer, so I thought—my husband thought—it might be nice if I gave you some special help.  Just to make you feel more at home, y'know."

This Mrs. Burnross is not at all elderly.  In fact, although she is the mother of young Zachary, she is quite youthful appearing, with long limbs, pale lipstick, and blondish hair swept back gracefully.  I must remember Mum's admonitions.  And her voice is rather high and perhaps strident.  The stridency may be accounted a typical Balonism, as I have discerned it in many Balona women, Mother Crinkle included.

"How do you propose being of help, Mrs. Burnross?"

"Well, first of all, you could call me Pippa."  She blushed prettily.  "And I suppose then I might call you Simon?"

"Of course, Pippa."  We chuckled together.  Mother Crinkle watched our intercourse from behind her *Courier*, a scowl on her face.

"I intend to vote for you, Mr., uh, Simon."

"Well, that is encouraging.  You are the first person to have declared her intentions, Pippa!"

Mother Crinkle snorted.  "That ain't true, Mr. Burberry, honey. I declared right away, when I first heard you was running."

"Ah, of course.  Well, since we are so close, perhaps I am taking you for granted, dear lady."

Mother Crinkle's scowl disappeared and she rustled her *Courier*.  "By the way, Pippa, you better not let Bapsie hear you're voting for Mr. Burberry here."

"Yes, yes, Billa. I hope you don't think me too forward, Simon, but when I decided to do something for you, I went ahead and called Buddy Swainhammer, the talk-show host over at KDC-FM? He's an old Balonan from way back, and he jumped at the chance to interview you. But I told him you'd have to approve first, of course."

"Why, how exciting an opportunity. I might be able to discuss my agenda over the airwaves, d'you think?"

"Oh, yes! And Bapsie Kuhl will be livid."

"Yes, I daresay. Well, what do you think I should include in my agenda?"

"The first thing, of course, is to convince your listeners that you're flexible."

"Flexible. Yes. I shall make a valiant effort to do that. And I do thank you from the bottom of my heart for your commitment— uh, to good government!"

Mrs. Burnross tittered all the way out the door. Mother Crinkle sneered. "Her husband is too old for her, y'know, so she's always unsatisfied." Mother Crinkle snorted and sniffed. The sniffing is indeed an irritating habit which she indulges even throughout morning coffee.

I gave Madog two days to recover and then visited him in his hospital room. Nurses twittered in the hallway, as I had brought a box of chocolates to the nurses' station when I inquired after Madog's room number. Mum always drummed it into me that the best way to cover one's bum, as Mum put it, was to be sure you had an unobstructed way in and out. And the quickest way is always with flowers for the prisoner, the patient, or the employer; and candy for the guard, the nurses, or the foreman.

Madog was in a room with several other men. His head was bandaged and his eyes were closed. I drew a chair up to the side of his bed and spoke in a low voice. "Madog, old fellow. How are you."

The eyes opened, brightened. The head moved and Madog at once groaned and frowned. "Oh, sir! There's two of you then."

Of course, I thought he was referring to the effects of the blow to his head. "No, no, I'm only one here. It's your concussion speaking, I should imagine."

"No, no. I mean to say, sir, it's you, Mr. Blade, sir, but you don't look like Mr. Blade until I looks right at you, y'know."

Madog's voice was raised somewhat, so I pulled my chair closer and spoke in lower tones, helping him to become calm.

"My name is Simon Burberry, old man." I put my hand on his forearm and squeezed briefly in the Balona manner. Madog appeared alarmed at this familiar gesture.

Then he at once assumed his usual crafty expression. Lowering his voice and leaning towards me, he whispered, "Ah. I see, sir. You can count on my discretion, sir."

I had never heard so many *sirs* from Madog. The usually sirless fellow must be after something, I thought. I went straight to the point of my visit.

"I need to know why you are in this country, and why you have been searching for me. Is it Mr. Tudwick's doing? Has he sent you after me?"

"Mr. Tudwick? Oh, no, sir. Not by any means. Me and Blight, we thought if we could get to you first with the good news, well, maybe you'd take pity on us and keep us on, instead of firing us. Times are hard for the likes of us at home, y'know. Have you seen Blight, sir?"

I thrilled to the sound of his words. *Good news*, he had said.

"Yes, well, I shall certainly consider your proposal. Now, why don't you tell me exactly what it is you wanted to say."

"Yes, sir. Well, I been just wondering how I'm paying for this hospital room and all the nice nurses and the clean sheets. They got no national health service in this country, where all you have to do is walk in the hospital and they pay for everything, y'know."

"Oh, don't worry about it, man. They have a way of taking care of indigents here. Nothing to worry about, y'know."

"Oh, but sir! With you as my employer, I shouldn't have to worry, correct, sir?"

"I am hardly your employer, Madog."

"Oh, but sir. You are now. That's part of the good news."

"Hmm? I don't understand."

"Ah. I am the first then, to bring the glad tidings."

"What glad tidings, man?"

"My Lady Demelza disappeared, as you may recall, and no one knew where she had gone to. Everybody was looking for her."

"Yes, yes. I knew that."

"And Mr. Tudwick at first thought her and you had run off together."

"Yes. You say, 'at first thought'? He no longer thinks that? It is not he who has sent you?"

"Him? No, sir, since my Lady Demelza has gone into a convent, y'know."

"A convent. Lady Demelza."

"Oh, yes, sir. Probably a convent. I seen the letter myself where Mr. Tudwick crumpled it up and threw it down. She has told Mr. Tudwick to get lost and has disappeared into God's Work, she says. And she has left her entire fortune—lands, manor house, stables, all that, and her bank accounts, too—to guess who?"

"To that fat little toad, Mr. Tudwick, of course."

"Oh, no, sir. That's the other part of the glad tidings. Mr. Tudwick is totally out of the pictue. My Lady Demelza has gone and left all to you! Me and Blight have came—on our own expense—to bring you the tidings, sir. You are a rich man, sir! And my beloved employer!"

# 26
## Joseph Oliver Kuhl

Me and Zack went snooping by Mr. Burberry's garage again, since Zack is sure Mr. Burberry is some kind of gourmet looking for weird dishes. Also, Zack is kind of jealous of Mr. Burberry, since Zack's ma is always talking about him and making public speaking arrangements for him, et cetera.

For example, Aunt Pippa found out from Mr. Burberry that he likes flowers. He suggested that back in England he was thought to be a pretty good gardener himself.

"At home I have a nice plot next to the stables," she said he said, "where I frequently dig for pleasure."

So she got Mr. Burberry to do a speech for the Delta City Garden Club. His speech title was "Using Blood-and-Bone-Meal to Make Your Garden Grow." This title Zack said sounded suspicious to him.

I don't think it was suspicious, since blood-and-bone-meal is a fine byproduct of King Korndog, where Mr. Sly is always joking about how, "We like profits and we don't waste nary a moo, a bleat, or a squeal!" So of course you have to pay for it, and it isn't cheap. Everybody around here forks a few sacksfull of the stuff into their gardens every year, since our regular dirt is mostly adobe clay, and you have to loosen it up to get anything to grow in it.

Our snooping at Mr. Burberry's garage was *open snooping*, since it is never healthy to snoop on a secret agent, even if you're not sure the guy is an active secret agent.

We got up to the driveway and heard whistling coming from the garage. It was Mr. Burberry's favorite tune. I have made that deduction from the fact that it's the only tune I have ever heard Mr. Burberry whistle.

"Hey, Mr. Burberry," I hollered, since the Crinkle garage door was about thigh-high open and we could see Mr. Burberry's thighs in there, the backs of them anyway.

The whistling stopped, the thighs turned around, and the garage door came up. Mr. Burberry was wearing his brown apron, but he still had his coat on. He was making another box. There was a big enamel pot on the hotplate. The pot had a lid but it didn't look like he was cooking anything.

"Hello, boys," he went, all cheery like. "I imagine that you might care for something thirst quenching from my new fridge." Actually, it had stopped raining, but the temperature was chilly, and we weren't particularly thirsty. However, Balonans are said never to refuse a free drink, and me and Zack proved the point.

Mr. Burberry has got a big new refrigerator set up in a corner of Mrs. Crinkle's garage. Before we could answer, he reached in and got a couple cans of Hires, my favorite, if not Zack's. Mr. Burberry opened and closed the fridge door so quick we couldn't see inside, which made Zack twitch a little, since he was hoping to see some interesting gourmet treats inside there. A jar of sheep eyeballs, maybe, or a huge, gross cow's tongue.

Right away I went, "We heard you on Buddy Swainhammer last night. You were pretty suave." I was hoping to oil Mr. Burberry up good and maybe get another job out of him.

"What you keep in your fridge, Mr. Burberry?" Zack always gets right to the point, but he also managed to change the subject to where he wanted to go. Just like Zack.

"Why, I keep nothing much in it yet. You'd like to take a peek? It has a lovely ice-maker and a veggie crisper and a large freezer compartment. Here." And he opened the doors so we could see stuff inside, some Valentine-candy-size square packages, some Halloween-pumpkin-size round packages, all wrapped up in heavy brown paper and tied with green string.

"Ah, you got any gourmet meat in there, Mr. Burberry?" Zack is pursuing the interrogation. "I understand you're a gourmet."

Mr. Burberry raised one eyebrow, an act he performs a lot of. He looked surprised at the question. "Gourmet meats. Yes, of course, and greens and spices and some of my construction materials, chemicals and glues—just to keep them out of the way, y'know. We always do that in Britain, y'know." Mr. Burberry smiled his lips and closed the fridge door. "You mentioned the talk show, Joseph." Mr. Burberry was getting the conversation back to where he wanted it to go, which shows he read his Manual carefully, or else he was angling for another compliment.

"Yeh, you did pretty suave, suavely." I repeated my compliment, since it never hurts to repeat compliments, whether the guy deserves them or not.

Mr. Burberry showed his teeth. He's got pretty large teeth, I noticed. I wrote the fact in my notebook which I carry in my bomber jacket pocket: *Burberry, large teeth.* This will help when down the road of existence I write my memoirs and need to deconstruct this part of my life.

"Yes?" Apparently Mr. Burberry was waiting for more scoop on his talkshow performance.

"Well, I dit'n actually hear it myself." Mr. Burberry's face fell. "But I heard about it from a bunch of people who said you were great." His face rose up

Zack went, "Well, I stayed up and heard the show. I thought Buddy Swainhammer sounded like an idiot, asking you if you believed in the Constitution. As if you should know anything about that."

"Oh, but I answered the question, didn't I!"

"You referred to the British Constitution. Sort of made Buddy look like an idiot, but he didn't realize that, probably, him being an idiot already."

"I hope I came off sounding like a viable candidate."

I wrote *viable* in my notebook.

"I notice you write in that little book every once in a while, Joseph."

"Yeh, I keep a vocabulary list of words I want to look up and remember. Sort of a habit."

"Good fellow. Good habit. Have that habit myself."

"Trouble is, after I write 'em down and then look 'em up, I forget 'em."

All this time, Mr. Burberry was smoothing a piece of wood with a little plane. Every so often he would hold it up to the light and measure it with a little ruler. He was smiling to himself. "Yes, there are things we should forget. Of course, with some things, it's not possible."

"That's for a new box, Mr. Burberry?"

"It's the beginning of another box, yes. It seems I cannot stop making them."

"Well, they're sure nice looking. They're all the same size."

"Yes."

"And the same color."

Mr. Burberry's eyes sort of flashed and he turned and said in a loud voice. "They *need* to be the same size and color."

"Okay, I dit'n mean to get you excited about it."

"Sorry, Joseph. I am passionate about my work, y'know."

Zack horned in. "I guess Mr. Madog it'n a secret agent, after all, huh!"

"Madog? A secret agent? Hardly." Mr. Burberry snorted in his nose.

"I guess since now he's out of the hospital, he must be over at Mrs. Splinters's place, taking care of it for you."

"Madog? At Mrs. Splinters's place?" Mr. Burberry glanced at the big enamel pot on the hotplate. "No, Madog has gone home. He had work to do, y'know. Yes, gone home." Mr. Burberry smiled, not showing his teeth this time, and returned to smoothing his board. He began softly whistling his tune.

"Hey, Mr. Burberry, you keep whistling the same tune."

"Yes, a lovely tune, isn't it!"

"It sounds familiar, but I can't place it."

"It's a theme from a symphony."

Zack horned in. "It's also a song that's got words."

"Ah, yes, that, too."

"So, you got Mr. Madog out of the hospital and sent him on home?"

"Yes, Zachary, that's exactly what happened. The poor dear fellow had received quite a lump, y'know, and—having done his duty to me—he was desperate to get home."

"So he came over here to help you out."

"Yes, Joseph, he brought me glad tidings from home."

"Well, honk. It dit'n sound like glad tidings when he was in Balona the first time." Zack sounded cynical.

"Madog explained all that to me. His explanation was touching." Mr Burberry took a piece of fine sandpaper and began sanding his piece of board. "He brought me the news that I am needed at home, for legal reasons."

"Aha!" went Zack. "You're wanted by the law?"

155

Mr. Burberry snorted, threw his head back, and laughed in his nose. "Ha ha ha! Certainly not, certainly not. It is I who am to contact the law over there, so that I might benefit from certain fiduciary arrangements that have been made in my behalf."

I wrote *fiduciary* in my book, Mr. Burberry spelling it out for me.

We said our farewells and took off for my house, me going on about how stylish Mr. Burberry is, Zack mentioning that the packages in the new refrigerator looked suspicious to him, and Harley growling and wagging his head, as if he hadn't believed a word Mr. Burberry had said.

We went to our house so Zack could pick up my ma's Krown, which had been damaged years ago, and which my ma now wanted to wear for Sugarbeet Festival. My ma was in the middle of a nap, so she groused a lot when she had to go search for her Krown.

"It's not too beat up, so it shut'n cost much to fix, right?"

"Well, A'nt Bapsie," went Zack turning the thing over in his fingers, "This thing is plastic. I thought it would be sort of gold or something. It's just plastic. See here? This part's practically falling off. I don't know if it's even fixable."

My ma's face dropped over the edge and fell about a mile. "Oh, no. You got to fix it. It's the only thing in my whole life that's got any meaning any more. Y' know what I'm saying? I mean, you got to fix it!" My ma said that mouthful like she was in church, not like she'd bust Zack if he didn't do the job. She talked about *meaning in her life.* I didn't know she ever thought about anything like that. She sounded like one of the characters in her soap operas. I was impressed that she didn't use one cuss word.

Zack's eyes got beady, which means that maybe he was setting Ma up. "I can try, A'nt Bapsie. But even if I can't fix it, it'll cost you $20. In advance."

"And worth every penny!" Ma dug into her cleavage and hauled out a bill. Didn't bat an eyeball, didn't try to weasel Zack out of his fee. "Here, you good boy," she went. "Put my Krown in this box here, so you don't let anything fall off of it."

So Zack took her beat-up Krown, like it was a famous royal jewel and put it in an empty frozen korndog box, carried it off across the street to his house, holding the box in front of him like it was a holy thing.

When we got inside his place, he took the Krown out of the box and twirled it around his finger. "First thing, I'll heat it up a little and see if I can bend it. The star here is all squashed, and the round part is flatted up. But I bet I can fix it."

We took it up to his room and he got his soldering iron out and messed with it on the Krown. First thing was, the star melted. "Oh, honk!" he went. "Oh, well. I'll try something else." The something else melted practically the whole Krown.

"Hey, Zack, my ma will grab you by the hair and throw you down our front steps, you don't fix her Krown."

"Forget it. Stay suave. I'll make her a new one. Better than the old one. One she can sit on and it won't squash. I'll put *two* stars on it. No extra charge. Right, Harley?" Harley nodded, jumped up on his new window seat stage and looked out the window.

While Zack worked on the new Krown, I thought about the tune Mr. Burberry kept whistling. Finally, it came to me. The song is called, "Going Home." I guess Mr. Burberry is a sentimental guy after all.

# 27
## Simon Burberry

"Have you any advice for a candidate, Mr. Keyshot?" I am asking my counselor this key question in order to ensure my victory, for the election is next week, on Tuesday following the weekend Sugarbeet Festival.

"Well, let's see." Mr. Keyshot scratches his ear, then his chin, then his scalp. "What do you think, Lamont?" The dog does not even open its eyes. "Well, probably you'll need to enter the talent competition."

"That should be no problem, for I do have considerable talent." I was actually being modest, for I am indeed multi-talented. "I could sing, dance, play the mandolin, or whistle. Which would you suggest?"

"Given the circumstances and the nature of your competition, I would say the whistling sounds like a good idea."

"What competition might that be?" I could not imagine any Balonan besting me in any whistling event.

"Mrs. Applehanger is sure to enter her birdcalls."

"Oh, well, birdcalls cannot hold a candle to truly competent human whistling."

"That may be, Mr. Burberry, but all Sugarbeet Festival competitions are for what is known as *open talent*; that is, it's the effect you create that folks are going to judge. There is no category. You will likely be compared not only with Mrs. Applehanger's magpie imitation, but also with Constable Cod's shouting. Cod usually wins the shouting match. Zachary Burnross has often won the juggling, and Claire Preene's flute playing is matchless. And many more folks perform on all kinds of instruments. One of the Delta Doodle Dandies won the chugalug contest a couple of years ago because he was able to drink down ten bottles of Valley Brew in four minutes."

"My word!"

"Yes. Well, the temperance people were scandalized, but the judges were flexible anyway and awarded the winner a case of brew which he finished before the evening was out."

"Well, I shall surely try to do my best whistling on that occasion."

"Don't strain anything practicing. I must emphasize that there isn't any real competition. Each of the categories is unique. That is, you enter and you have created your category and you win. Of course, you are donating some of your boxes. That surely will make a nice impression." Mr. Keyshot shoots me a keen glance. "Are you feeling well? Your face is ruddy and your eyes are very bright today."

"Ha ha ha," I chortle. "Yes, I am doing as well as can be expected for one necessarily dining at Frank's Soupe de Jour for three meals a day." I have been hoping Mr. Keyshot would give me such an opening.

"How so? Is Mother Crinkle feeling poorly?"

"Mother Crinkle has, shall we say, disappeared, dear thing. Of course, she has left me her power of attorney, executed some days ago by Mr. Kenworth Burnross, so I shall continue paying the utilities, and so forth. But as far as I know, she may now be serving the needs of the children of Nicaragua."

"I wasn't aware that Mother Crinkle had a philanthropic bone in her body." Mr. Keyshot reddens, places his hand over his mouth. I recognize the gesture as exactly the same as one I myself had made here some days ago. Mr. Keyshot rarely says a discouraging word about anyone, but Mother Crinkle once was his mother-in-law and reportedly served him the same medicine with which she dosed Madog.

I need to explain the disappearance. "Mother Crinkle and I were watching a program on the telly some nights ago, and she was taken with those little children who were facing crises in their lives. 'I should go down there and help those little tykes,' she said. Her eyes were glistening, she sniffed constantly." I don't mention to Mr. Keyshot that the sniffing was a truly maddening habit, but as a former resident of the Crinkle abode, Mr. Keyshot is surely well aware of the sniffing.

"Remarkable, really remarkable. Well, I'm happy she has come around to helping those in need."

"At any rate, she has failed to leave me a forwarding address, so I'll just have to bash on as best I can." I give, I hope, a creditable impression of a loyal basher, bashing on. "Speaking of helping those in need, when she finally shuffles off this mortal coil, she intends to leave me all her property, y'know. Or did I already mention that fact?" I crinkle my eyes and nod my head, showing my appreciation of Mother Crinkle's benefaction.

"I didn't know you had become so, uh, close. Y'know that Mitzi, her youngest daughter, is likely to have something to say about property disposition."

"Oh, I'm not a greedy sort. I'll be happy to settle out with any and all of her children—when the time comes. Of course, this conversation is quite premature for, despite any Nicaraguan jungle terrors Mother Crinkle may experience, I'm sure we'll see her dancing the streets of Balona again."

"Your interview with Buddy Swainhammer was interesting." Mr. Keyshot has changed the subject and his tone is neutral. Is he complimenting my performance?

"I thought I responded rather well to the questioning." Mr. Keyshot does not respond to my assessment, instead asks me if I wish to have a cup of tea. "Surely, and with thanks," I reply. So much for the Buddy Swainhammer experience.

"So, you will be speaking and participating in the talent show. Will you sponsor a booth?" Mr. Keyshot's question is one I had not anticipated.

"A booth?"

"Sugarbeet Festival offers opportunity for citizens to sponsor booths at which food, crafts, and other items might be sold, the proceeds from which are donated to the Sugarbeet Fund."

I plead ignorance of the Sugarbeet Fund.

"That fund is given over to the Mayor to help pay for projects at his discretion. Or her discretion. This year the discretionary item is hoped to be the installation of a second light pole on Front Street. That accomplished, we may be able to make our way all the way down the street to Airport Way without getting lost in the fog on the trip." We both have a laugh about that.

"Of course, I shall sponsor a booth. My booth will offer raffle tickets, and the prizes shall be my boxes. They're already on display, y'know, in Mr. D. H. Carp's windows downstairs.

"Fine, fine. Those boxes'll create a lot of stir, and probably sell a lot of tickets, too. Excellent." Mr. Keyshot leans over and scratches the ears of his sleeping dog.

I think about the boxes. Mr. Keyshot continues to scratch. I consider angles, hazards, opportunities, cautions. "I should probably ensure that winners of my boxes do not try to open them."

"Oh? Why's that? They're puzzle boxes, after all. I'll bet that's the first thing your winners will try to do."

"Oh, they must not. There are reasons."

"Well, then, you'd better display those reasons publicly and prominently, right there at the Sugarbeet Festival."

"A sign, perhaps. A prominent sign, explaining, yes. Yes, I should do that."

"Patrick Preene could print you up a poster."

"Splendid! Yes, I shall have to state the reasons clearly."

"Oh, my yes. If I won a puzzle box, the first thing I would want to do is to solve the puzzle and open the thing up."

"That could be disastrous. The reasons are, are, well, the reasons are complicated. Let's see. There is the glue I use to assemble the pieces. That glue is of my own manufacture, but when it is exposed to the air, it becomes lethal."

"Then your boxes are not designed as puzzle boxes after all?"

"Well, the puzzle part is for my amusement while I'm building them, you see."

"Ah." Mr. Keyshot's response signifies that he does *not* see.

"I shall have the sign say something like, *Do not try to open, as in the process of manufacture, certain chemical glues were employed that when exposed to air may cause severe lung, kidney, liver, and brain damage to anyone who inhales nearby.*"

"Yes, your sign could say that. My experience tells me that if the winner is a teenager or someone over 65, the attempt may be made anyway, for teens and seniors sometimes feel that cautions on labels and signs do not really apply to them."

"Very good point, sir. I shall add something like, *In addition to death, serious acne, incurable bad breath, and shrunken gums are some of the inevitable results of inhaling the glue fumes from inside the boxes. Do not drop. Boxes for display purposes only.*"

"Excellent. That should keep them at a distance." Mr. Keyshot frowns, "As you feel you must keep them at a distance."

Because we have heard no sounds on the stairs, the loud rap on the door takes us both by surprise. "Yoo-hoo!" The voice is that of Mrs. Shaw. "Anybody in there, boys?"

Mr. Keyshot looks at me. I raise my shoulders and remark, "It's all right. It's fine."

"Come in, Bell."

I rise quickly, but Mrs. Shaw seats me with a grand gesture.

"Well, I just saw Mr. Burberry from my office window, y'know, saw him coming up here, and I thought how nice it would be to have a nice cup of tea with my two favorite boys." Mrs. Shaw is wearing a blue running suit, very large white basketball shoes, and is carrying a furled umbrella with a heavy curved handle, possibly the door-knocking instrument of choice. She titters and keeps me in view while she circles Mr. Keyshot's chair.

"Well then, Bell, why don't you do the honors with the tea!"

Mrs. Shaw rummages at the sink. "Has Mr. Madog recovered from his wounds, Mr. Burberry, uh, Simon?" It seems that everybody in Balona is aware of Madog's injury, his stay in the hospital, and his recent recovery.

"Yes, he is recovered nicely and has returned home."

"He's gone already."

"Gone home. Yes."

"Like Mr. Blight." Mr. Keyshot resumes his ear scratching, the dog still sleeping.

"Gone home, sir, like Blight. Yes. Except that Madog will be doing me some favors." I decide to accelerate the news by means of Mrs. Shaw whose *Courier* column many Balonans read. "I may as well reveal all, Mrs. Shaw, uh, Bellona, as it will soon be public knowledge. I am in the way of receiving a fortune at home, as my former employer has passed on, leaving me a considerable estate."

"Law! Is that a fact. Passed on, you say."

"Did I say 'passed on'? I meant to say 'passed into another life,' the religious life, I meant to say."

Tea making is put on hold for the moment as Mrs. Shaw draws up a folding chair and sits next to my knee. "Does that mean you are withdrawing from the election? From the race against Bapsie Kuhl?"

"No, indeed. I shall participate in the Sugarbeet Festival and the election, and after the election I shall return home to settle my affairs. Then I plan to return to Balona and assume my office." I show my teeth but cannot take my eyes from Mrs. Shaw's lipstick which is of a purplishly vibrant red. I am beginning to tremble. Mrs. Shaw blushes and returns to her sink.

"Well, now, Mr. Burberry, you sound optimistic indeed."

"Yes, sir. I feel optimistic. Everything is going my way. I can feel it in the air." If only I could find my keyring.

# 28
### Joseph Oliver Kuhl

Next to Christmas vacation, Halloween, Fourth of July, and end-of-the-school-year, true Balona guys like Sugarbeet Festival most. This year is no exception.

The holiday always happens in the spring, when green is just starting to poop out on the trees, and the Yulumne is either really low and sad-looking or is already juicily crashing by with icy snowmelt from the Sierra. This year, however, the Town Council decided to have it earlier. So we're having our good old festival the weekend before election day, the famous day when my ma will or won't become Mayor of Balona.

It didn't rain for a couple days, so most of us true Balona guys helped set up booths for the various exhibits and stuff. The place is of course my Uncle Hannibal Chaud's Funerals parking lot, since it's got lights. The only other place with lights is Pezmyer's Buicks, down at the end of Front Street. Being as how Uncle Hannibal's is across the street from Frings Bowls means when you get tired and thirsty from your pre-Sugarbeet Festival labors, you can go over there and get yourself a Hires. Of course during the Festival, there is all sorts of stuff to eat and drink right there in the parking lot. Also a lot cheaper than Frings.

Me and Zack decided we would help set up Mr. Burberry's booth, where he is stacking his boxes to show them off during the raffle. We agreed to do this for a foreigner as part of our civic pride, even though it's a rich foreigner.

"You're sure my boxes won't be rained on?" Mr. Burberry looks after those boxes like they are chicks and he is a mother hen. He has checked on them and re-arranged them several times a day in Mr. D. H. Carp's windows, Mr. Sackworth says, worrying about temperature and light and whether there was any dust in the air. He was mostly worried about rain that might fall during Sugarbeet Festival. "Even one raindrop would render the finish blotchy, and then, who would want a blotchy box?"

We agreed that probably box blotch was the worse thing in the world. So Zack went and got a couple rolls of plastic stacked up behind Mr. D. H. Carp's Groceries & Sundries, apparently un-owned by anybody. We have stapled the plastic over the top of the booth so, even if it rains, the boxes should stay pretty dry.

We told Mr. Burberry, "There's no guarantee that it won't rain and blotch up your boxes. But it probably won't." It was Zack put it that way, not exactly the least worrisome way of saying it. But then, Zack continues to be suspicious of Mr. Burberry, saying that Mr. Burberry has got something to hide, only Zack hasn't figured out yet what is being hidden.

I think since he's now sort of a partner in King Korndog and has probably got lots of business worries, et cetera, Mr. Burberry is just struggling with the problem of having life's problems piling up on him.

As a student striving toward excellence in my chosen field of Criminal Justice, and as a fellow striver with Mr. Burberry for superior performance in my chosen dream of being a secret agent for MI-6, I sympathize with Mr. Burberry's flight. Since I am more sophisticated than my high school cousin, and know more psychology and life and stuff, that is natural. So, there you are.

To give an idea of how Sugarbeet Festival works, it's a bunch of booths around the edges of the parking lot, with a stage built up in the middle. This is the famous stage where the contestants strut their stuff. (*Strut their stuff* is an expression a guy hears if he hangs around Mr. Keyshot, who uses it all the time. It is not a native Balona expression.) Since everybody stands all around the stage, the performers have to turn around a lot during their strutting so everybody can see their backs as well as their fronts.

Balonans dress up in costume for Sugarbeet Festival. If you don't dress up you are considered un-suave. I have appeared as Humphrey Bogart (an old time movie actor). Once I came as a korndog, but nobody recognized my homemade costume as such and guys accused me of looking like a turtle, which could be constrained as sort of an insult since the Fruitstand High School Turtles are rivals of the Balona High Noble Korndogs.

A while back, a whole Sugarbeet Festival got washed away. But that's not likely to happen again, if I can keep my dad in his booth at Frings, drinking coffee and watching out the window,

instead of practicing on the Yulumne River levee bank with the
Balona Volunteer Fire Department's high-pressure hose.

For this Sugarbeet Festival I dressed up as a religious monk,
wearing a beat-up old brown robe with a hood I got at St. Vincent
de Paul's Thrift Shop for a dollar. The robe looked familiar and
smelled sort of ripe, but I think I look really authentic in it, except
for my suave fashion place Air Jordans, which really ought to be
bare feet in ratty sandals. Zack came as an injured football player,
wearing his oversize motorcycle helmet and his neckbrace and
staggering around on crutches. When Mr. Burberry showed up we
were disappointed because he came as himself, wearing his
raincoat, his black hat, and his wraparound shades. "I am a
candidate," he went, even though he looked like he was waiting
for a martini stirred, not shaken.

But even Mr. D. H. Carp showed up in costume, wearing a
slick shiny green evening gown and a red wig. Mr. Burberry
started looking at Mr. D. H. Carp like he was going to strangle the
poor old guy. However, we diverted his attention to re-stacking
his boxes and refining his booth, and making sure each box had its
Certificate of Authenticity signed by the artist. Mr. Burberry had
also got this huge sign printed up over at the *Courier* that told you
how you'd better treat the boxes right, if you won one.

"I want to be sure everyone sees and understands the
conditions of ownership," he went. "I wouldn't want anyone to be
injured. Or die." When he mentioned *die*, we took him seriously
and passed the word around that the boxes were safe only if you
didn't try to open them up. I can't imagine anybody opening one
after all the warning. The sign was huge and we tacked it up so
everybody could see it who even got close to the booth.

Of course, there's always my little brother Richie, who will
usually do whatever you tell him not to do. But fortunately,
Richie is out of the way for a while, him already being back in
Runcible Hall on account of certain crimes and misdemeanors I do
not wish to elaborate about at this time.

Also, when selling his raffle tickets, Mr. Burberry had each
buyer sign a pledge that he wouldn't try to open his box, even if he
won one, which wasn't likely. The reason it wasn't likely many
guys would win was that me and Zack volunteered to check the
tickets and had fixed the drawing in advance so just the right
number of guys would win. That was just to avoid confusion, not

for any crooked reason. Besides, each of us wanted one of the boxes for ourselves. Zack was already figuring out how he could open his up with out breathing in the noctuous fumes. His only problem, he said, was Harley, because Harley wanted to witness the opening.

Anyway, the competitions had to wait until the Noble Korndog Band marched around and played too many pieces, old Mr. Langsam waving his arms until it looked like they were going to fall off. Everybody clapped, though, and Mr. Langsam bowed more times than necessary, until it looked like he was going to fall down from exhaustion. As a musician myself, a trained percussionist who does not ply his craft much any more, since my ma gave away my drumset, I can say that the band has improved some since I trod the halls of my alma mater.

Then the Korndog Flag Fems, also from Big Baloney, came marching down Front Street and swaggered into the parking lot, poking and waving their flags, with Bootsie Dwindle throwing her baton up in the air and dropping it a couple times, and then weeping to the cheers of the audience.

After that, while guys were eating their cold-storage french-fried sugarbeets from little bags, the entertainments started, with Constable Cod beginning the shouting contest. Actually, for a real fat guy, Cod has a very loud voice. You don't often hear it since he's usually eating and wheezing, but when he goes after an evil-doer, you can hear him from Front Street all the way to the dump. The only other guy who competed was Coach Kork, whose voice is a lot higher and wispier, so there was really no contest. Everybody applauded, though, and both guys got prizes, since that's the way you keep the peace in Balona.

Then Mr. Burberry had the drawing for who would win his boxes. He first of all had to make a speech in which he repeated about not trying to open up one of his boxes. He mentioned pimples a couple times, since that's one of the results you will get if the fumes from the boxes get to your skin. Lots of guys, especially girls, shuddered at the thought.

Me and Zack won our boxes, of course, and Mr. D. H. Carp (the fix was in). And we thought Mr. Keyshot and Mrs. Shaw ought to win one each, too, so we fixed that. They had bought raffle tickets like everybody else, so that worked out fine. The other boxes went to respectable Balonans who *ooohed* and *aaahed* about the nice craftsmanship and the high-gloss finish and the general beauty of the boxes.

Mr. Burberry went over to each winner and had him raise his hand and swear an oath. Each winner had to take good care of his or her box, not drop it, not shake it or leave it sitting out in the sun. And to keep it out of the rain so it wouldn't get blotches. There was some horsing around, and a couple of winners joked like they were about to drop their box, but when they saw Mr. Burberry's expression on his face, they soon stopped that.

Mrs. Applehanger got hoisted up to the stage and did her imitations. She did magpie, jay, and blackbird, and then she threw in meadowlark, which she had never done before. It was pretty impressive. For an encore, she did chicken, which everybody appreciated, since her rendition had the chicken in its egg-laying mode.

Lots of other guys did their thing. Nothing great.

Mr. Burberry followed at last, and when he finally got up on stage to do his whistling his lips were probably dry. You couldn't hear much, since the tune is pretty low. Me and Zack tried to calm the audience down so everybody could hear, but guys still kept laughing and carrying on, so Mr. Burberry didn't look pleased.

Then Mr. Burberry stayed right up on the stage and started off his election speech with a trope that surprised everybody.

*"How's things, neighbors?"* he went. Suddenly there was this huge silence. Even the Noble Korndog Band members who usually puncture every speech with noises blown through their mouthpieces stopped their clamor. The Delta Doodle Dandies held off chugalugging out of surprise.

Then, everybody at once hollered back, like a choir making its crescendo, "How's things, Mr. Burberry?" Then, we all cheered like crazy. Mr. Burberry was finally a true Balonan.

Mr. Burberry right away went into his election speech, which came off pretty suave, since he spoke in a loud voice like Shakespeare and mentioned just about everybody in the audience by name. This is another trope that people really like, and showed that Mr. Burberry had done his homework and deserved to be mayor. He got a lot of applause.

Then what happened next, still causes my skin to crawl and my bladder to shrivel up. My ma appeared, wearing her repaired Krown. Everybody cheered, since they knew if they didn't cheer they'd each hear from my ma, one way or another. She was barefoot, of course, and had our green garage raincoat draped over her shoulders. She was carrying the top of a garden torch. She lit the torch with the lighter my dad used to use when he smoked. My crawling skin and shriveling bladder wasn't because of the coat or the Krown or the torch or even the bare feet. It was because of what happened next.

Ma got into sort of a pose, raised the flaming torch, and let the coat drop to the stage. There was a loud gasp from the crowd, but nobody could say a word.

My ma, Bapsie Chaud-Kuhl, candidate for Mayor of Balona, had something filmy draping her otherwise naked boobs, but not much, and she was wearing a *thong*. That's all that was covering 240 quivering pounds of flesh. She hollered, loud as Cod at his best, "Vote for me, Bapsie Chaud-Kuhl, and you'll get more'n you bargained for!" And she twirled the torch like Lady Liberty, did a little dance, and pranced around on that stage so all could get an eyeful of the rear as well as the front.

The Delta Doodle Dandies, all of which had participated in the Valley Brew chugalug contest, gave a huge cheer. The Sugarbeet Festival pretty well broke up after that.

# 29

### Simon Burberry

An excellent piece of advice from Mr. Keyshot had me at Mr. D. H. Carp's Groceries & Sundries just as the store was opening on election day. Mr. Carp and Mr. Sackworth had already set up the voting booths and I, as first at hand, got to vote for myself without comment from anyone.

The voting process is simple. One signs the register, takes a ballot, marks an X in the box before the candidate's name, and deposits the ballot in the ballot box next to Mr. Sackworth's cash register. Presumably, the votes are counted after 7:00PM, at which time members of the Town Council take the box upstairs to the Council Chambers to count the ballots.

I stood at the meat counter in hopes of greeting customers and pressing more flesh, finding that station to offer admirable stimuli for my endeavour. Mr. Carp keeps his knives excellently well sharpened, a steel close by his block. I watched him slice some ham for Mrs. Applehanger, the birdsong imitator, who said that she regretted not winning one of my boxes but that she intended to vote for me anyway. Mrs. Applehanger warbled and twittered as she waited for Mr. Carp to complete his slicing, testament to constant practice as a necessary component of any skill.

At about 10:00AM, after 20 or so customers had passed through the store, and I had reminded each of the opportunity to vote for me, Mr. Keyshot and his black dog entered the store. The dog was on a leash and, although the weather was clear, Mr. Keyshot was wearing a raincoat and a knit cap down over his ears. The dog also wore a raincoat, in a manner of speaking, plaid fabric covering its back and held on with straps. Mr. Keyshot greeted me effusively.

"Best of good fortune to you, Mr. Burberry!"

"Thank you, sir. I intend to win this contest."

"That you probably shall do! Would you care to join us in our constitutional?" He meant for me to join him and the dog in his morning walk.

"I hesitate to leave my post, sir," I explained.

"Well, perhaps I might explain something, if you were to allow yourself to abandon that post for a while." He crinkled his eyes and spoke very pleasantly, so I regretfully left my station, just when two more customers were entering the store.

"As a rather competitive person, I wish not to be gone for long, sir." Perhaps my tone reflected my peevishness.

"It's just that I need to tell you something that perhaps would be better said in private."

I donned my trenchcoat, scarf, hat, gloves, and dark glasses, and we strode out of the store, my attire perceived as especially cosmopolitan, I'm sure, by the several women customers who witnessed our departure. We headed south on the Front Street sidewalk.

"What is it, Mr. Keyshot, that is so important that I should leave my post at this significant time?"

"A simple matter of law, Mr. Burberry, which you could not have known. It is illegal for candidates to so closely monitor the voting as it proceeds, as you appeared to be doing. Also, it is considered unethical for candidates to campaign within so many feet of a polling place. I knew that you, a man who has described himself as a *compulsively* law-abiding person, would wish to be told." The dog stopped us as it sniffed at a fireplug.

"Ah!" I was truly aghast at both my crime and my ignorance of the law. I could feel myself blushing. "Ah, I must have misunderstood your advice about being early at the polling place? What shall I do, then? I feel compelled to continue campaigning."

"I am sorry that I didn't make myself clear. I meant only that you would do well to vote early. I was of course joking when I said, 'vote early and often.' That's an old-time American jest."

"It's a British jest, too."

"To remedy the situation, I should think you would need to do nothing more than desist from campaigning in that particular place. Perhaps you could station yourself at Constable Cod's bench. It's distant enough to offer you plenty of public visibility, yet not impinge on the voting processes themselves. I'll bet Cod wouldn't mind at all, especially if you brought him a few sacks of popcorn."

"I could wave at the voters and shout greetings."

"You could shake hands and kiss babies."

"I wouldn't have to shout."

"You could speak in normal tones, converse with Cod and with Frank's customers, wave at people coming and going from the variety of Front Street businesses."

"And I would not be violating the law! I would be strictly legal, yes? I would not wish to violate the law in any way."

"You would not be violating the law."

"Ah, Mr. Keyshot, you have been my rescuer." Now it was Mr. Keyshot who blushed.

We continued our walk all the way past Frings Bowls (where one could hear morning bowlers rumbling their sport) to Ned's Sportsbar (through whose swinging doors one could already discern the odors of beer and spirits and the happy cries of morning imbibers), then crossed the street and returned.

"Is it legal that Ned should be serving spirits this early in the day? There are no 'hours' for public houses? Doesn't the Constable make a scene about that?"

"Hm. There you have an example of the flexibility with which Balona treats its citizens."

"I see. As mayor, I shall be expected to support this degree of flexibility."

"Of course."

"I see." Such flexibility has its merits. As mayor, I shall become the very model of a flexible Balona mayor, but I did not mention that happy fact to Mr. Keyshot.

My advisor and his animal continued their trek to Balona Park for health reasons. As I turned about to make my way back to Mr. D. H. Carp's Groceries & Sundries to purchase popcorn, I noticed a large black-and-white bird, a magpie, perched on the street-side corner of Kenworth and Joseph Kuhl's office roof. The bird seemed to curtsey at me. I lifted my hat in greeting.

At Carp's store, I was informed, "We don't stock popped popcorn, Mr. Burberry. But we got carmelcorn, which Cod likes better." Mr. Sackworth perceived my intentions without my having revealed them. "I guess you're wondering how I figgered that out? Well, you don't look like the popcorn type, and I seen you and Mr. Keyshot there pointing at Cod's place, so I figgered it out, see?" Mr. Sackworth beamed.

"You are on target, sir. How many carmelcorn packages are recommended for this mission?"

"I would say five, Mr. Burberry. Five will be the satisfying number."

171

I took the shopping bag of carmelcorn across to the Constable's office. Constable Cod was just returning from Frank's Soupe de Jour with a Franksburger in his hand. His small eyes lit when he saw my gift. He invited me to sit and join him at his bench outside the constable's office. "It's a dice thing to noo, Mr. Burberry. You are sure a nice guy. So that means you will probably be our next mayor, which is okay with me."

For much of the rest of the day, except for lunch at Frank's, the Constable and I greeted citizens as they passed. I waved at those across the street. Most waved back. Most smiled. I did not bother to make an issue of Mrs. Kuhl's posters in the windows of Mr. D. H. Carp's Groceries & Sundries. It appeared to me that I had the election *in the bag*, a phrase Balonans use frequently.

At about 4:00PM the constable looked up from his snacking and observed, "Well, whaddya know! I do believe I seen that feller before!" His gaze was directed at a man staggering in this direction from Ned's Sportsbar, a disreputable appearing person, quite in his cups from all appearances. "It's Card Splinters! Hey, Card, we thought you was in Montana!"

"Montana? Hell, no. I been drying out in Arizona. Never been in Montana in my life. Never been rich, either, but I could use a job, get me back on my feet. Where's my ma gone to, Cod? Anybody know?"

Constable Cod introduced me to Mr. Splinters. I took pity on the fellow, obviously in need. I offered him a job at King Korndog.

"Hey, I'm qualified chopper hopper operator over there."

"So I have heard," said Blade.

# 30
## Joseph Oliver Kuhl

Anybody in Balona could've told you Mr. Burberry would win the election. But my ma wouldn't believe it when Mr. Carp came downstairs and announced it to the crowd gathered on Front Street to hear the news. Ma demanded a re-count right then and there, and then went upstairs and sat in and helped count herself. Naturally, she "found" about a hundred ballots marked in her favor that hadn't been counted.

Mr. Carp said the ballots "looked homemade" to him, and he thought Ma had brought in the extra ballots under her muumuu. Ma reported to us that right then she was about to throw Mr. Carp down the stairs by his hair, "but he dit'n have enough hair to grab onto." Anyway, Mr. Carp hid under the table up there until she decided to leave. But even after all Ma's efforts, Mr. Burberry won. He is the new Mayor of Balona.

Now Zack has made it to my ma's list of un-favorite persons. She is convinced that Zack's makeover of her Krown is what did her in with the voters. The next person on her list is my dad, who didn't support her enough, she says. "Richie wut've supported me," she sniveled. First time I ever heard her sniveling while sober. She was mentioning my little brother when she named Richie. He is a guy who is my ma's favorite kid, since he is fat like her, but nowhere near as tall. Richie looks a lot like my Uncle Anson and even has the same lisp. Of course, Richie's not around.

So now Ma says she needs to recover her self-esteem which has been damaged. She's got my Grandpa Daddy Kon Chaud to give her a trip to Hawaii as a victory present. "He don't need to know I lost," she went. Grandpa Daddy Kon is a resident of the Jolly Times Rest Home down on First Avenue. They are always threatening to kick him out of the Jolly Times because of his "unspeakable behavior" there. But he's rich, so that counts a lot.

"Who're you gonna take along?" went Mrs. Earwick, my ma's househelper.

"You wanna go? You could sit on the beach and drink while I carry on. They like big women in muumuus over there."

"Sure," Mrs. Earwick hollered. So that's who's going in a couple weeks: My ma and 98-year-old Mrs. Earwick, who doesn't get around too fast, which is a condition my ma is probably counting on.

"I don't get to go?" went my dad.

"You dit'n support me is why," went my ma.

So that's that. Me and Dad will have to make do.

Mayor Burberry offered Dad a job over at King Korndog, since lately they're always needing guys to work over there and Mr. Burberry is in charge of hiring. But Dad declined the kind offer, he said, because he doesn't like the smell.

The smell over there is great when they open up the ovens, but in the daytime it's pretty awful. Mr. Sam Joe Sly takes off for other places as often as he can, but Mr. Burberry says he likes it. "I like the general environment here," he says.

Mr. Burberry offered me a job, too. He said I could work part-time, and at night so it wouldn't interfere with my classes, and I'd make a pile of money. I could maybe get Card Splinters's job, he said.

Mr. Burberry gave Card his old job back, but then Card took off again, leaving a good job without notifying anybody. Probably in Arizona, says Cod. Probably in Montana, says Mr. Burberry, gone home.

But I don't know. I actually prefer standing around at Mr. D. H. Carp's Groceries & Sundries where you can watch the girls go by and get paid for doing practically nothing.

Mr. Burberry is going back to England to collect his fortune over there, he says. "I'll be back soon," he went to Mrs. Shaw who wrote about it in the *Courier*. "After all, I cannot leave my constituents for long, can I!"

Me and Zack dropped in on Mayor Burberry's garage where he was working on his new box. He seemed happy to see us, which he isn't always. He even pointed to a sack on the floor near the door where Harley could flake out while we chatted with the new mayor.

"Hey, you're working on another box!" we mentioned.

"It is what I do, you know. I have an inner voice that tells me, *make another box*, and so I do." He showed his large teeth.

"We each of us got us one of your boxes, y'know," I mentioned. "Mine is heavier than Zack's."

"Mine is shinier and smoother." Zack always has to have something better than you.

"I hope you will take to heart my prohibited behaviors regarding your boxes."

"Oh, yeh. We signed the thing, the agreement. We know. We're gonna take good care of it. I got mine on my dresser where I put my Aqua Velva and my pimple cream on top of it."

"Well, under the pimple cream and Aqua Velva you might want to put an antimacassar, to ensure that the finish of the box is preserved." I guess I looked blank, so he clarified. "A doily."

Zack went, "I hear you've also inherited Mrs. Crinkle's house here, Mr. Mayor. That's convenient."

"Yes, well. Mother Crinkle continues to bless me, y'know. I hope she's doing well down in Nicaragua, giving help and succor to the little poor children down there. Probably. A fine lady." Mayor Burberry doesn't pronounce Nicaragua the way Blip Wufser pronounces it on *Blip Wufser and the News*. Of course, if you don't watch the news much, the way I don't, it doesn't matter how Mr. Burberry pronounces it.

Zack went, "I hear you went and gave Card Splinters his old job back, but he took off again."

Mr. Burberry gave Zack a hard look, then smiled with his lips. "Yes, it is so presumed. Took off again. Gone home."

"I hear he said he'd never been in Montana."

"Well, I suspect Mr. Splinters's memory and perhaps other functions have been affected by his habits, and that probably he has been with his mum and simply not remembered. He most certainly is with her now. Poor fellow." Mr. Burberry is actually a very sympathetic guy. You can tell from the way he looks when he talks.

"Is that lacquer you're putting on there?" Zack is always interested in crafts and stuff.

"It's actually a plastic material." Then he went on to explain how he mixes this and that. I wasn't interested and started to look around when suddenly Harley stood up and stared toward the house. There was noise in there, like the TV just clicked on.

Mr. Burberry put down his brush and went and opened the garage door. He wagged his head, looked sort of worried. "I hope your animal has sharp teeth, because it appears I may have a burglar."

I grabbed a hammer and Zack picked up the hatchet. We sneaked into the back porch, Harley leading the way, Mr. Burberry behind us. Just as we got to the back door I began to think that maybe Mr. Burberry ought to be in front and us in back. But Zack went and turned the knob, pushed open the door. It sounded like a chicken house going on. (So, like Patella's always saying, I'm *sexist*. A chicken house is exactly what it sounded like.) There was Mrs. Crinkle and a couple of other ladies, including Mrs. Crinkle's daughter Mitzi, all of them talking a mile a minute, laughing and carrying on.

"Hey, Mr. Burberry, honey. Look who brought me home from Delta City where I been visiting. It's a few of my daughters. They all wanted to meet my new boyfriend. Hello, Joseph. Hello, Zachary. I don't like dogs in the house." Mrs. Crinkle gave Harley a hard look and he crept back of us, a discreet dog.

"Honored, ladies," went Mr. Burberry in his Shakespeare voice. "Hardly 'boyfriend,' I'm only your mother's humble roomer." He bowed his head and looked suave. "Welcome home, Mother Crinkle. We thought you might be in Nicaragua, didn't we boys?"

"Yeh, that's what everybody heard," went Zack.

"Ah! Am I too late to vote?" Mrs. Crinkle looked worried.

"Mr. Burberry is already Mayor Burberry of Balona," I went.

"Well, it'n that grand!"

"But he's going back home for a while to get richer, except then he's coming back pretty soon."

"Well, I hope so. Balona needs him. He's got such style!" Ω

South Lake Tahoe, California 2001

# More Balona Books

Besides **The Burberry Style,** Jonathan Pearce's other published "Balona Books" to date include

—from Infinity Publishing
(www.BuyBooksontheWeb.com)
call toll-free 1-877-BUYBOOK :

**The Balona Klongs:** A Demi-mystery Caper
**Finding Dad:** A Quasi-mystery Adventure
**Focusing the Private Eye:** A Mysterious Term Paper
**One Brick Shy:** A Hemi-semi-demi Mystery Adventure
**Spring Break:** A Wet Adventure
**A Cuisine of Leftovers:**
Stories and Sketches of Eminent Balonans
**Thing with Feathers:** A Different Romance
**Heavier than Air:**
Riches to Burn in Balona
**The Far Side of the Moon:**
A California Story
and
—from 1stBooks Library
(www.1stbooks.com):
call toll-free 1-800-839-8640

**John-Browne's Body & Sole:** A Semester of Life
**Sang Froyd:** Capers of the Balona Family Kuhl
and
**A Little Honesty:**
Trials and Triumphs of a Prince of Balona.

Balona Books are *POD*—printed and bound on demand (printed when ordered). All these books are available *through* any local bookseller who will do you the courtesy of ordering for you, by phone direct from the publishers (quickest!), or from Amazon.com ("Balona Books"), or through the
**Balona Website:** http://www.balona.com.

Lightning Source UK Ltd.
Milton Keynes UK
UKOW03f1907220713

214199UK00018B/1378/A